Red Horse Radish

Herman Edel

authorHOUSE®

AuthorHouse™
1663 Liberty Drive
Bloomington, IN 47403
www.authorhouse.com
Phone: 1 (800) 839-8640

Published by AuthorHouse 10/12/2015

ISBN: 978-1-5049-5574-4 (sc)
ISBN: 978-1-5049-5576-8 (hc)
ISBN: 978-1-5049-5575-1 (e)

Library of Congress Control Number: 2015916750

Print information available on the last page.

This book is printed on acid-free paper.

Chapter One

Iasi, one of the most gracious cities in all of Romania, has been famed throughout Europe since the mid-fifteenth century. It is pronounced Yash.

Soon afterwards, a number of Jewish families from all over Europe started arriving in Iasi. They found it to be a safe and welcoming community.

Yes, through the years there were Pogroms that brought much harm and killings upon this ever-growing Jewish community, but, on the whole, Iasi provided a pleasant homeland for all.

Several Jewish doctors begot much fame as being superb practitioners of their trade. Wealthy people with a variety of illnesses from all of the nearby countries flocked to Iasi for their services.

Small businesses and agriculture were the prime occupations for Jews. Some of the more ambitious became vintners for the grapes and, therefore, the wines were quite good.

As early as the mid-sixteen hundreds, Iasi had become a regrouping place for people who were trying to reach Eretz Yisrael. Many of these travelers found Iasi to be a good place to live in and thus the Jewish population slowly grew in size.

The beginnings of our family started when one Jewish couple surfaced in Spain early in the Second Century. They were treated as the lowest of people by the Spanish people and even their fellow Jews who had preceded them in this new land.

They were called by all as 'gente sin valor' which in Spanish means people without worth. From there the name Sinvalor evolved and later the 'vitz' was added by a particularly cruel Spaniard who wanted all to know that this group was just another bunch of worthless Jews.

Through the years, no one bothered to alter this slur of a name. In time, it was held as a proud symbol of how they had survived the vilification it implied.

Like all Jews, they clung to a life that was filled with harassment, suffocating taxation or just plain slaughtering. But somehow they survived and became of the same value as any Jew in hate-ridden Spain.

In the 1400's a new law called the Alhambra Decree was enacted. It had the strong backing of Queen Isabella. The law all but guaranteed total expulsion or death to any Jew living in Spain.

Now Sinvalorvitz is hardly a noted name, but in those years it carried great weight because of a Jew named Don Asser Sinvalorvitz. The story of this man was passed down from generation to generation.

If there was a leader of the Sephardic Jews in those troubled times in Spain, it was Don Asser. This outspoken, but brilliant, man was listened to by both Jew and Christian alike.

Even Queen Isabella felt kindly towards this little Jew. That affection lasted for a brief period but when he rose to scream against her favored edict, the Alhambra Decree, and seemed to be gaining support against it, by Christian as well as Jew, she issued a simple order.

"This Sinvalorvitz bothers me. His rallying against our Alhambra Decree is bothersome. I can tolerate his fellow Jews screaming out against it, but he seems to be gaining some support from non-Jews as well. Put him and all his family to death as soon as viable."

One of the favored officials in the Queen's inner circle owed much to Don Asser. As a long term friend, he would not allow his friend and family to face any such edict.

Within a week, over forty eight members of the Sinvalorvitz family, led by Don Asser, were gone from Spain. They quietly settled in various European countries. It was only in Romania that they kept their Spanish surname.

Some four hundred years later, it was decreed by my great grandfather that the world was ready again for the name Don Asser to be carried by a proud Jewish boy. Oddly enough this new Don Asser turned into a carbon copy of the original carrier of that name.

Asser Sinvalorvitz, my grandfather, was that man. He died long before I was born, and I would not have known anything about the man if it were not for the fact that the man I idolized, my Poppa, Schmuel Sinvalorvitz, never stopped telling me story after story of his hero.

First of all he was five feet ten inches tall. This made him akin to a giant among a family where five feet and two or three inches was considered respectable.

Yes, he spent a good deal of time on his father's stature, but he spent much more time telling us how all in Iasi bowed to the intellect and moral strength to Iasi's Don Asser.

Don Asser spent his life moving a small men's store that he had inherited up to the stature of an important Iasi business. So did the stature of the 'Tall One.'

To all intents he was the leader of all the Jews in Iasi and when some trying matter arose in Iasi, Asser Sinvalorvitz played a major role in settling the problem.

His stature rose when he wisely purchased a number of farm lands that produced superb grapes. His wines became among the most popular in Iasi and his wealth soared.

Very few people in Iasi sported two such widely successful businesses.

Schmuel, a rather skinny and short man adored Asser and made certain that each of his children knew everything about that uniquely grand man. His favorite quote about his father was, *"Dat vas a mensch. A guta neshuma."*

Which in English meant a grand man in soul and heart.

"He took over der famila's zer klaine men's clothing store ven he vas stil a boy and made it into a richtik business. Dat vine business vas an equal success. He made everytink about Iasi vonderful for us."

May I introduce myself? My name is Dieter Sinvalorvitz. I was born in the good old U. S. of A., but my Poppa and Momma were born in Iasi, Romania.

It didn't take me many years before I started complaining about my dreadful first name and the fact that I wasn't given a middle name. I eventually did change my first name but my Poppa squashed any thought of a middle name when he simply said, "Ve are poor, and ve can't afford a middle numen."

That didn't make any sense to me, but Poppa was Poppa, so I just accepted his edict.

Of course, I couldn't understand how they were so rich in Iasi and so poor in New York.

"Vas it his fault dat tings vent crazy In Iasi? Foist they took away his farms. Den dey stopped buying in our store and ven dey started killing off the Jews he led us to America. He died too soon to make America like the old Iasi but to me he vas alvays mine Groiser Roes.'

Should you have had any trouble interpreting the above, may I offer the following advice, look at it as being the best efforts of a terribly insecure group of people trying to communicate with each other.

Much in this book will feature a combination of Yiddish and tortured English. As my people aged, the Yiddish slowly disappeared.

For the longest time a 'w' was almost always pronounced as a 'v.' They were more comfortable with a 'd' than a 't' and 'that' was spoken as 'dat.'

Thus 'where we were born' would emerge as 'ver ve vor gueoirenboren.'

My parents were quite proud of how quickly they had picked up this foreign tongue. No one ever told them otherwise.

If needed, I suggest you might first enjoy trying to decipher the meanings yourself or use the lexicon decipher I've placed at the end of the book.

Yes, there are also translations scattered throughout the book which might also bring you a chuckle or two.

Be kind to their pathetic attempts to verbally reach out to you. It is not so much that they used different words for they thought they were using 'poifec' English.

Chapter Two

The Sinvalorvitz family, led by Asser, was a pride to both Jew and Christian. Asser's greatest joy was building his business. He did it remarkably well. Their men's clothing store grew in size every year of it's over one hundred years of existence in Iasi.

Asser's wine business was amazingly rewarding.

The Pascal's, on the other hand, lived from week to week. They were relatively new to Iasi. Duvid Pascal was a milkman who had no care or thoughts other than enjoying every moment of the day.

He was rather happy-go-lucky. However, as handsome as can be and the charmer of every Jewish girl in Iasi, he delighted in his own fame.

Both men had the good fortune to meet the twin sisters Yettie and Sarah Veiss at about the same time. And thereby meet one another.

Yettie's romance with Asser was praised by all, and their marriage was the social highlight of the following year.

Duvid fought off the wit, charms and beauty of Sarah for some years, but Sarah knew that Duvid was the man for her and Duvid knew there was no such woman as good as Sarah.

Yettie was the first to deliver a baby boy and continued apace, while Sarah tarried awhile before a beauty named Molly sprang forth with a smile and a temperament that caused love to pour down on her during every day of her life.

Despite the almost uniform distrust of Duvid, both marriages could not have been happier for the grooms and the wives. From the first moment he met Sarah, he never even glanced at another woman.

Poppa knew all about his father, Asser, and Momma did the best she could about Duvid Pascal, the father she loved with an undying passion.

Though always in need of more money, the Pascals smiled away almost every day of their life together.

Despite the financial differences between the two families, they remained very tight. Asser enjoyed the joie de vive of his brother-in-law, Duvid, who in turn reveled in the brain of Asser.

Isadore, a fierce little baby, arrived exactly ten months after Yettie and Asser were married. Then, in rapid order came four girls, Pessel, Gittel, Malke, Lisa, a longed for boy, Schmuel, and finally Sophie.

Five years later in America the Sinvalorvitz's had two boys, Eli and Itzhak. Eli emerged as a typical lower East Side aggressive youngster.

On the other hand Itzhak's life was forever filled with sordid disdain for the troubles he constantly fought in this cruel world. Later in this book we'll go into that life.

It took the Pascal's three years before they had the beautiful and very smart, Molly. Two boys, Chiam and Schlomo soon joined this very happy family.

Chapter Three

The word love is a strange thing to understand when you are young.

When Schmuel Sinvalorvitz was two years old, love had no meaning whatsoever to him but he liked touching his newborn cousin, Molly, who was the daughter of his mother's sister. His little sister, Sophie, who was born two months earlier than Molly, was never touched by Schmuel.

At the age of four, Schmuel found it difficult to distinguish between his sister, Sophie, and Molly, but he did know that Sophie was a little older and a lot bossier than Molly.

He also knew that he didn't want his sister around when Molly was in his house. He and Molly could play all sorts of silly games without Sophie, who was always in charge and constantly changing the rules. He thoroughly enjoyed being alone with Molly.

His one older brother was always nice to him and he felt good about that. His four older sisters, who were always fussing over him and kissing him, he didn't like at all.

When he was six, he stared playing a new game with Molly and Sophie. The game had been invented by Sophie.

She would lie on her back and Sam had to lay on top of her. He didn't much like the game unless he was lying on Molly. They didn't play that game very often.

At about the same time, Schmuel was dubbed with a new title, 'The Quiet One.' Truth be told, he was always quiet. He seldom spoke to anyone. His head was always filled with thoughts, but only rarely did he open up to others. He knew that he enjoyed being quiet, for then he did not have to disagree with anyone.

Furthermore, he was more than content to continue to debate with just himself. He did not need outside comment.

His mother was very concerned about his infrequent talking. When she queried teachers at both schools that he attended about his being so quiet, they both responded in the same manner.

"It is very strange. When asked a question in class he can hardly get a word out, but when he is given a test he always gives the best answers."

Chapter Four

At eight years of age Schmuel was ushered to his father's shop and introduced to the tailoring department. This was a tradition that his father and many father's before him had undergone.

That one day each week contributed to what was now known as a fine menswear shop.

There was no discussion about this decision. Everyone but Schmuel considered it an honor that had just been bestowed on the boy. Regretfully, he knew it meant even less time with his favorite friend, Molly.

Within months, they started teaching him the craft of being a fitter. He soon realized by being a fitter, the man who sized up how to cut the cloth to best fit the man and the suit, led to your being the leader in the tailoring room.

To his utter amazement, he slowly found that he enjoyed that work. It became obvious to him that if he had to suffer this loss of freedom, he would become the best fitter in the world. In later life he did just that.

As he grew older, going to school dominated his life. Each morning from eight A.M. to one he attended a small City School.

From three P.M. to five P.M. Schmuel, and most of the other Jewish boys of the neighborhood, attended the Cheider, the Jewish School, where only Hebrew and Yiddish was spoken. Because of its far larger size, it had more to offer its students.

That space was in the basement of Schmuel's family's house. They did not charge anything for its use.

Both schools had one serious problem -- its teaching staff at the lower grade levels was far from adequate.

In the Iasi school, this was shown at the end of the very first day in class. Schmuel and the boy seated next to him nearly leapt out of their chairs when their teacher told both of them to listen up.

The following was directly contrary to school rules which forbade placing Christian boys with the inferior Jewish boys.

"Starting tomorrow morning, you both will come to school an hour earlier than everyone else. You will find several paper bags on my desk. You will then go to each of the classrooms on this floor. You will pick up all the garbage or debris you find there. You will leave the bags in the last room after checking that the rooms are spotless. Do you understand your assignment?"

Normally, this could have been a gross mistake, but with these two boys it led to a friendship that was deep and important.

The Cheider on the other hand, had a young Rabbi as its teacher. This rather young teacher had a tendency to shout out to his students in Hebrew and then shout even higher, as he interpreted into Yiddish the words he had just relayed to them.

The young man, a tough nosed Ashkenazi Jew, had recently arrived in Iasi from Germany. This was fortunate for the Cheider had just lost its teacher. He was the most boring teacher Schmuel had ever experienced. It made being a student there all the more difficult.

Schmuel learned to drift through the lessons at Cheider by hearing what he wanted to hear and ignoring the rest.

Chapter Five

Early the second morning, the boys arrived at almost the same time. Not a word was passed between them as they scurried from corner to corner of each room and then returned to each room to be certain all the rooms were immaculate.

The second day they duplicated the efforts put forth on the first day but, by the end of the week, they had slowed their efforts considerably and still left the rooms spotless.

They worked well together, but, to say the least, they were not enamored of each other.

The event that brought them together was the day Dieter walked in carrying a book entitled 'Trails of Iasi.'

Towards the end of their chores that morning Schmuel asked if the book Dieter carried meant that Dieter liked to hike around the city.

"Why do you care?"

"Well I have taken just about every trail there is in this city."

"I don't think you have seen anything."

From this argument grew a friendship of grand proportions, as each boy guided the other to new paths the other one had not even dreamed of.

Within the next few months, Dieter and Schmuel were irrevocably bonded. Somehow, a boy of German heritage met a similarly nice Jewish boy. They never talked about the why's and how's of this friendship. All they knew was that each had found a friend they cherished.

Dieter took Schmuel on trails that lead to hidden vaults of wondrous old churches. Schmuel had never seen anything quite so woven with paths leading to and fro from each church. It opened him to why there were so many Christians in the world.

Trying to compete on that level, Schmuel took Dieter to a Jewish Cemetery that was reputed to be over one thousand years old.

For Dieter it was proof that the Jews had been in Iasi forever.

Both boys had been told by many people of the old adage that if you threw a brick anywhere in Iasi you would break a church window. They searched and searched but never saw a church with a broken window. Each also brought the other to mountains that seemed to soar through the sky or hidden little streams that wandered through dense forests. They delighted most in finding oddly built old houses that seemed to tell stories of an ancient Iasi.

Each trip opened up new excitement and wonder for the insatiable seekers of glories that the other one had never seen.

This almost daily occupation drew them ever closer to each other. They reveled in keeping the knowledge of their friendship solely for one another, as the friendship grew stronger and stronger with each passing day and was never revealed to anyone else.

They constantly assaulted each other with expressions like, "Oh yes. Well I can show you trails that you have never even dreamt of seeing."

With every new trail they took, each church or synagogue they visited, the bond between them grew in intensity.

Chapter Six

Both boys received warnings from their mothers who sensed a change in their sons.

"I never see you anymore. It's like you are off in some wilderness."

For which their excuse was how much work they had at their schools. The 'work' never ceased as their excursions grew more and more exciting.

All changed when Molly posed a similar question that complained of never seeing Schmuel. This led to Tuesday and Thursday being the only days for scouring through their city.

Schmuel drew a strong reproach from his father at about the same time Deiter received a similar bit of advice from his father.

'You should never even think about spending any time in the neighborhood on the other side of The Roiter Brik (Schmuel's father) or The Rota Brika (Dieter's father).'

Those words, whether spoken to Schmuel or Deiter, clearly indicated that this long and narrow bridge, which spans the Prut River, is the dividing point between people who honor you or detest you.

Each father ended the dictum by adding that the people on the other side of the bridge hate you, and you don't want to have anything to do with those dreadful people.

'Stay in your own area and both sides will be happier.'

The boys listened intently but totally ignored same. They roamed freely on each side of the bridge. And in the ignoring became much wiser and closer.

The one answer that completely eluded them was why the bridge was named The Red Bridge since there was nothing red on the bridge or anywhere in the neighborhood of said bridge.

One day they did not hike but spent the entire time trying to discover how and why their bridge was labeled with the word Red. After hours at the official library, they failed in their efforts.

The city school and the Chaider were located on opposite sides of the Prut River which the Roiter Brik spanned.

The river started in the southern hills of Romania. It grew larger by the time it reached Iasi and then coursed north between Romania's small neighboring country, Moldavia on one side and Russia on the other side.

Russia and Romania both laid claim to Moldavia, and a bloody battle was constantly being fought over said ownership.

It puzzled the average citizen of all three states, the common plaint amongst all three countries being simple enough, 'what the hell are we fighting for?'

Moldavia was by far the smallest and poorest of the three countries. The deficits of the country would soar whenever Romania or Russia decided to attack its little neighbor. The happiest days were when both countries left Moldavia to be owned by Moldavians.

Iasi was located in the North Eastern section of Romania and was the fourth largest city in Romania. It was considered to be the nicest city in all of the country. Its reputation as the educational hub of Romania was well earned. For one thing it boasted five outstanding colleges. It was the perfect place to grow up in for both Dieter and Schmuel.

Chapter Seven

It was late one evening and the Sinvalorvitz family had just finished yet another wonderful and plentiful meal that had become a tradition. Per usual, it was shared by the Pascals.

Molly and Sophie were seated next to one another with Schmuel, of course, seated next to Molly.

Both families were gabbing away as they stretched or yawned or tried to slip out of the big dining room when Schmuel's father, Asser, called out. "All of you please sit down."

What surprised everyone was that Asser spoke in Romanian. Each of those in the room knew that when Asser spoke like that something important was about to be told to them. Silence pervaded the room.

For some time, Asser merely sat there with a very somber visage but not looking at anyone.

Sophie, one of the youngest children there began to giggle but was quickly shut down by her mother, Yettie.

This brought Asser out of his reverie. He rose from his chair. It was a very stern man who looked out on the bewildered faces looking up at him. A little tear floated down both cheeks. He roughly brushed them both aside before continuing

"For you younger people what I have to say will be a huge shock. You may not understand why I have recently made a decision that is going to change all our lives."

The very tone in his voice shocked each and frightened every one of them.

Duvid Pascal, who had not uttered a sound all of the evening moved his chair next to Asser ready to endorse what had to be said.

"What is happening in Iasi today and every day is becoming worse and worse. We are being forced to do something that just six months ago I would never have dreamt of doing."

Not a sound was uttered in the large room they were seated in.

Normally, by now all would be astir as the dishes would have been cleared away by the older women. The youngest among them would be chasing after one another and much laughter would be heard from the others.

Duvid's wife, Sarah, kept dabbing her eyes with a handkerchief that was already soaked. She, sister Yetti, Isadore and Duvid were the only ones who knew what Asser was about to say.

"You will surely have many questions to ask me. You will certainly be puzzled and possibly be very angry at what I say, but please listen carefully and I will answer any questions you might have."

He looked at everyone in front of him. There wasn't a face that did not reflect total puzzlement. After a very long pause he began again. His voice was low but solid.

"In two weeks, Isadore, our oldest and most courageous son, will be leaving Iasi and traveling to New York City. He was told to do this after much discussion between Duvid and myself. After hearing us out he totally agreed to taking his family on this this masssive change in their lives."

Asser took a dramatic pause and then went on.

"His mission there is to prepare everything so that all of us can join him in America."

The uproar of approval shook every piece of silver and glass sitting on the large table.

"Yes, thank you for agreeing with what Duvid and I decided must be done. It was almost prophetic that we named our first son after his great, great, great grandfather who was the first of our family to move here from southern Romania. He was the man who brought the Sinvalorvitz clan here over one hundred years ago."

The shouts of hurrahs for both Isadores echoed through the room.

"Yes, plaudits to those who will now be leading us in this new adventure from Iasi to New York City, America."

He paused, as all the mouths facing him seemed to pop open, yet not a sound came forth.

It took many minutes before they regained their speaking ability and in place of silence a torrent of words erupted. It seemed like everybody was talking with the person next to him or shouting praises to Isadore.

Through all the ensuing noise Schmuel did not utter a single word.

"Please listen carefully to what I must now tell you. We are dispatching him to New York where a job as a tailor awaits him and living space will be open for him. We hope that his mission there will be a huge success for it will affect all of us."

Still very somber, he waited until not a word was spoken. Instead, all were staring up at him.

"I want you to know that I have always loved Iasi and will continue to do so. But things are happening in this city of ours that has forced Duvid and me to make a very difficult decision. Isadore's work in America will enable all of us to move from Iasi to New York City."

Nothing could repress Sophie at that point. She jumped up screaming out, "We are going to America."

She then danced throughout the room singing at the top of her voice those same words.

Her antics were applauded by everybody save for Schmuel, who sat in his chair with his hands folded tightly together. He glared at his father.

Asser solemnly nodded his head, as the mothers grabbed their children and forced them to quiet down.

"Schmuel, everyone has heard the same words and they all seem quite happy, but you are staring at me as if you hated every word I said. Do you have something to say?"

"I hope he enjoys himself in New York. When will the rest of my family be leaving Iasi?"

"That will take some time for him to do what must be done. Hopefully, it will not be more than several months before we are ready to leave."

After a very long pause he began again.

"In two weeks he and his family will be leaving Iasi and traveling to New York City."

"Let me now tell you what has driven us to that decision. It will not be an easy chore for any of us. And there are many difficulties involved in this move. We have already arranged to sell this house. Fortunately, the man who is buying it is willing to have us use the house for as long as we remain."

It was Asser's wife, Yettie, who now took over.

"One of our most difficult things to do is that for each person we take, we can only take two bags of our most treasured possessions. I beg that each of you, and that includes young and old, start gathering what you want. We must be ready to leave at a moment's notice."

And again Sophie screamed out, "I'm leaving everything here, and I'll buy everything new in America."

Frowning, Yettie sat Sophie down while admonishing her.

"Sophie, stop acting like a fool. We will have very little money at first. Tomorrow you and I will start packing."

Through all the ensuing noise Schmuel did not utter a single word.

Despite another very stern look from her mother Sophie jumped up and started screaming away. "We are going to America."

She then danced throughout the room singing at the top of her voice those same words. Her antics were repeated by just about everyone in the room save for Schmuel, who sat in his chair with his hands folded tightly together. He glared at his father.

Chapter Eight

Asser rose and walked to Schmuel's side and gently took hold of Schmuel hands.

For some time the two just looked at one another. The softness of this hand grasping was a sign of the affection one bore for the other.

"Poppa, do the Pascals mean to leave with us?"

"No, we believe it will take them more time to put together their needs for this trip."

Schmuel dwelt on that for a few moments and then told his father. "Well I think I will stay with them until I decide whether or not I will go to America."

"Don't be ridiculous. Of course you will leave when we all leave."

"Why?"

"You are leaving because I am your father and you obey what I have to say."

"Then I have a different question to ask you. Why are we leaving?"

"That is what I want to tell you. I have made a very difficult decision. Let me tell you what forced me into that decision."

Schmuel merely nodded his head.

Asser turned to all the others who were agog with joy.

"Please, listen up. Per usual my brilliant son, Schmuel, has posed a pertinent question. I want you all to hear the answer.

Again, his tone was so serious that even Sophie quieted down.

"We first came to Romania and then Iasi due to the intelligence of a man named Isadore and yes our Isadore was named after that man."

Laughingly, the current Isadore shouted out, "Don't expect that of me."

Asser ignored him as he continued talking of how brilliant the first one was.

"The man who brought us to Iasi sensed there was something special about this little village. His family arrived here somewhere in the mid- seventeen hundreds. They settled in an area east of the main section of the city. It was called 'kikevile.' To this day, calling someone a kike is an easy way to demean a Jew."

Asser paused as he looked at every face in the room.

After some time, he added a few proud words.

"That Isadore did one other thing of some value he opened a tiny tailoring store here which grew to be the store we are so proud of. That store has brought us many blessings. But, be aware. Those days of blessing are over."

It was as if a seriously wet blanket had covered the entire room

Schmuel asked a second question that re-awoke the sad family.

"Would he do what you want us to do?"

"I believe he would have to do so. And, I should tell you that the man who opened that first store was much like you."

"How?"

"That man was very wise and hard working. He, like you, was not a talker but very much a doer. Given the present problems we face, I feel certain he would have taken the same path."

"Do you think you are much like him?"

"No, not at all. He was a great thinker. I am a plodder compared to him. He had the courage to bring his family to Iasi so that their lives would be broadened. I must take them from Iasi in order to save their lives. Do you understand the conflict in those two statements?"

"Yes, Poppa, it means there once were a lot of smart people in Iasi who accepted the Jews who came here, but today there isn't much sympathy for the sons and daughters of those Jews."

The two just looked at one another for some time before the father released his son's hand.

"Let me tell you more. If after I am finished and you still refuse to follow the path I want you to take, I will allow you to do so. But first let me tell you the story of Iakov Psantir."

He then related the story of the first Jew to come to Iasi. He arrived somewhere between Fourteen Sixty-Seven and Fifteen Forty-Nine. Many Jews followed his lead. The first pogrom began in Iasi some thirty years later.

Asser stopped to ask Schmuel if he knew what a pogrom was.

"Yes, Poppa. It is when the leaders of a country decide to massacre many, many Jews."

"Almost correct. If they had their way they would kill all of the Jews. But the first pogrom in Iasi did not kill many Jews. First of all there weren't many of us here, and, secondly, they were all slaves anyway."

He then went on to describe the many pogroms that followed and the fact that whenever things became economically difficult, the Jews would be stripped of their holdings and all their wealth taken from them.

"It is a plague which attacks the Jews of Europe with some regularity. We are leaving because it is beginning to do so again here in Iasi."

He continued with a legendary story that had been passed down through the years. It revealed how crazed the enemies of the Jews were.

There was a Prince Mihai who early one morning had an old and very wealthy Jew named Lieba to be taken to the front of a popular synagogue.

Lieba kept crying out one question.

"What do you want from me?"

He never received any answer but, for the impertinence of asking the question, the rulers flogged him even more with whips while demanding he stab his son and shed his blood.

In Yiddish he kept whispering to himself the hope that he would be dead before he performed such an act. That prayer was soon answered.

The fury exhibited by Mihai's men so stirred the masses watching this passion explode that they got into the joy of it all by destroying many Jewish homes and razing every Synagogue in the area.

Of course all of Lieba's funds were appropriated by Mihai.

Observing all of this was yet another Romanian noblemen, Prince Constantin Mavcordat. He was unique as he looked upon Mihai's actions with much disfavor. He had several laws issued that favored the Jewish population.

Unfortunately, his brother, Prince Ioan Mavcordat, took the opposite position. He simply extorted large sums from the Jews and then forced them to buy a certificate to bring a ritual slaughterer to their homes.

Schmuel was even more confused.

"Poppa, I do not understand this at all. First we are left alone so we rear great scholars and the finest doctors and a happy people who quietly do well for themselves and their families. Then, from out of nowhere someone says, 'Let's go kill some Jews.' Why poppa, why?"

Asser openly wept as he drew Schmuel up and kissed him repeatedly.

"My son, you are almost thirteen, and I have just celebrated my fifty-first birthday, yet I am no closer to an answer than you are. I could tell you story after story that is far worse than the Lieba story, but I cannot give you any words that make sense of normally decent people deciding that once again it was time to torment the Jews."

Schmuel started shaking. He grasped his father's body. He looked up into the face of the man and hoped to hear answers that could take him through life.

Father and son fell to the floor. The older man, hating himself because he couldn't come up with the words his young son needed -- the younger adrift with no hope for the future.

"Schmuelila, you heard the worst but now you must focus on only one thing. We can, no we must, flee this land as soon as can. We must start again in America, and we can and will survive there. Think not of the past but only of what is ahead for us. I want you to believe that a great future is out there awaiting us."

"But, Poppa, I hear you say things that frighten me so much. Will I live long enough to give my Bar Mitzvah speech? Are things so bad that we will all be killed so that crazy people can take everything we Jews have. Will the Pascal family survive because they have so little?"

And, with tears flowing down his face he added "Will Molly be murdered because she is pretty?"

His head was aswirl with thoughts of things that ended with innocent Jews being slaughtered.

"Poppa, why do they hate us so much? Are we Jews really bad? Certainly we don't rule anyone. I don't see us stealing anything or harming anyone. Who decides it is time to kill the Jews?"

Asser then explained the economic disaster Russia and Poland were now wallowing in. Their leaders had to find a scapegoat for their past avarice and stupidity.

Voila, they distracted their citizens by reopening the noble tradition of Anti-Semitism. Kill the Jews and then take all their assets and all will be well again.

The Jews who could flew to a hopefully peaceful land. This time they chose Romania as their safe haven. In retaliation to this invasion Romania burst into their own hellish pogrom.

"But Poppa, we are not Polish or Russians so..."

Schmuel was whipped. He couldn't understand killing another being to get that person's wealth. Even a stranger thought was did they kill Jews just because they were Jews.

"Poppa, I don't understand."

"Schmuel, I don't either. But we have a choice. Stay here and be killed or flee to America and try to begin a new life."

With a deep sigh, Asser told his twelve year old of his giving much money to several important leaders in the hope of thus satisfying them, but nothing seemed to satisfy their greed.

He had just been told that his pride and joy, the clothing store, was to be sold for a paltry sum.

"But they stupidly made one mistake. They also forced me to also sell our wine business. The price is at a ridiculously low price. But if we add the two amounts together, we will have just enough for us to buy our way out of this country and into America. We must cling to that one chance."

He did not tell his son that when all was said and done and they were safe in America, they would be penniless.

"But how do we know it will be any better in America?"

"At least nobody there will be trying to kill us."

"Poppa, am I right in saying we must leave Iasi?"

"No, we must fly from this country. We have only one choice and that is to escape from certain death. If we intend to keep this family alive, we must leave this country as soon as possible."

Chapter Nine

Schmuel nodded very solemnly. He was very confused and then a thought stared buzzing in his head.

"Poppa, if we had another child in our family couldn't we bring her with us?"

"Of course."

"Then, why can't we bring Molly with us? She and Sophie could be sisters. They look and act like twins and with as big a family as we have, who will notice one more little girl?"

Poppa stared at his son. He was dumbfounded at how simple his son's thought was.

Later that night he laid out this additional plan before both families. Many tears were shed but all readily agreed to the pure genius of it.

Molly fiercely objected, but her father reasoned that her going was an additional bonus for the entire family. Now all the other Pascals could afford to move to Paris which could give them more time to raise the money necessary to get to America.

"Molly, sending you now will enable us, with God's help, to be together all the sooner."

Schmuel was praised for his idea. His father's accolades made him feel like a real 'mensch.'

His Aunt Sarah, normally a non-emotional woman, grabbed him and smothered him with kisses while whispering in his ear, "You are going to be the smartest tailor in all of America."

For the first time in his life, Schmuel felt what being in love meant. He was in love with everybody. He even loved the crazy Romanians who were causing his family to move to America. He could not think of any place to which he would rather go.

Both families started an intensive effort to learn the English language. The children seemed to grasp it much more quickly than the adults.

Chapter Ten

Dieter was particularly happy on Sunday afternoons when he kissed his mother, swore he would be home early for this evenings dinner, kneeled his last kneel of the day, and raced out of the church.

Yesterday afternoon he had finally discovered how to get into the tunnels that circulated through much of Iasi's underground. This would top anything that Schmuel had ever seen.

He raced to the Rota Brika, knowing that his friend, Schmuel, would be there to greet him.

Per usual, they would meet in the middle of the bridge, and, since Sundays were always Dieter's turn as leader of the day, he shouted out, "We are going to the best place ever and…" but then he stopped.

Schmuel was not looking at him but stood there with his face hidden behind his arms which were buried in his chest.

"Hey, Schmuel, are you sick or something? Come on, what kind of game are you playing on me today?"

"I guess you could say I am sick but, no I am not sick. I have something to tell you that may make the both of us sick. Dieter, before I say what I must say, you must swear that you will never repeat it to anybody."

"Oh come on Schmuel. What are you trying to fool me into this time?"

"Dieter, Dieter, you are the only one I can tell this to, and I must repeat that you can never tell anybody what I am about to say."

"Okay. Schmuel, I will never, never tell anybody what you are about to tell me, and I will never again eat the Pastrami you gave me last week."

Still Schmuel hesitated. Could he trust his best friend with this awful news? There was little doubt in his mind but that he must.

"Dieter, last night my father told the entire family that soon we will be leaving Iasi and moving to America."

Dieter looked intently at his friend and then burst into a very loud laugh.

"You know, I think you should become an actor. You had me there for a second but, I know you better than that. So we've heard your funny story, and now can I tell you what I have in store for us today?"

"I wish it was a funny story Dieter. But that's not the case. Last night my father told us of his plans to move us to New York City."

"Enough is enough. That is not funny, so just stop it."

"Dieter, please believe me. We are leaving Iasi forever! I hate the thought. I hate telling it to you, and I will forever miss you and Iasi."

Dieter backed away from his friend. The words he was hearing were quite distasteful to him. He could not put any sense of reality into what his friend kept repeating.

"Schmuel, tell me that you are making up that horrible story."

"I wish I could, but it is the simple truth."

Dieter had so wanted to dazzle Schmuel today. Desperately, he started muttering about the great day they would have today.

"....And those tunnels are... they are... they... When is this terrible thing going to happen?"

"I don't know but I think it will be sooner than later."

Both boys were now crying as Dieter put his arms around his very best friend and whispered, "I swear I will never tell anyone."

For the next hour they sat there without a word passing between them. People passing by would stare at the boys, and wondered what they were doing and why they seemed so sad.

It was Dieter who first stirred from the sadness.

"Hey dumb, dumb your stupid story made me forget what we are going to do today. I bet you haven't even heard of what I'm about to show you."

Schmuel bounced up, grabbed Dieter's cap and raced off with it all the while shouting, "You'll only show me anything if you can catch me."

What neither knew was at that very moment Schmuel's father had just handed over a sufficient number of lei's to finalize the trip his family would soon take.

The Sinvalorvitz family left Iasi forever in just short of two months.

Other than in school, Dieter nor Schmuel would never meet again, nor would they ever make so close and important a friend.

It plagued them for the remainder of their lives.

Chapter Eleven

Molly was intent upon keeping her family up to date on everything she was doing on this oh so long, long voyage away from them.

Accordingly, the first chore she undertook each morning was to write a letter to her loved ones in Europe. No matter that it could not be mailed, she numbered each letter in the hope that someday it would be received.

It was her way of staying with the people she loved so much. Eventually, each such letter was sent off.

The Sinvalorvitz journey took them first to Hamburg. It was just an overnight stay. Joyfully, Molly dispatched the first of her letters to her loved ones.

Two days later they were off to Dover, England where three days were spent before they braved the Atlantic Ocean.

The horrors of their days on the dreadful little boat they traveled on were beyond comprehension.

Their arrival in New York was greeted by Isadore, waving a large American flag and a smile that was large enough to greet all of those finally leaving Ellis Island.

Great joy greeted each of the family from the minute they moved into their terribly over crowded first apartment. Yes, things were far from perfect but each one pushed their ways into trying to become Americans.

The one who founded it the most difficult to do so was Asser Sinvalorvitz.

He was in his mid-fifties when he first began to doubt himself. For most of his life he had been a wealthy man and a leader in his community. His life was filled with family and civic activities. He was a happy man.

But now his lack of capability with the English language both plagued and inhibited him.

In these very neediest of days, he found it impossible to get anything going in this crazy new country. Without funds to invest in, he found himself solely relegated to very meager jobs.

This humiliation began to eat away at the man. In this new country, he was just another nobody trying to regain a status that he seemed not to warrant.

He took every little job he could get, but not one gave him any satisfaction and, instead, his self-regard disappeared.

At first he relied on his son Isadore to get him contacts that he could meet with or to advise him on what was happening in the clothing business and what he must do to get started in this new land.

Unfortunately, his son could not go beyond what meager knowledge he gained in his little job as a cutter in a woman's dress factory.

He contacted every former resident of Iasi who might know of him, but there, too, he discovered that they were barely surviving and were reluctant to help anyone who might become competitive to their own efforts.

Fear was rampant throughout these new Americans.

From there, he attempted to reach Jews who came to America at a much earlier time and, once again, found that they were having their share of just being able to pay the rent and put some food on the table.

It was the German Jews, all of whom had been in America for some time, who put the dagger in his dreams. Yes, he did speak German, but to them he was just another Romanian supplicant who could add nothing to their coffers.

Here was a man who, for his entire life, had been an important and admired figure. But in this new land, there was nothing but scorn awaiting him at every turn he took.

Handouts became his only source of income. The money came with many. "I' sorry Asser, but there is nothing more I can do for you. I wish you luck."

Finances got so tight that he had to recall a note from two of his best friends who had a small hotel in the Catskills.

The note was quickly repaid and almost as rapidly used to pay off daily debts.

This entire transaction tore at the soul of Asser.

It wasn't too long for the people, who in Iasi had coveted his relationship, now couldn't find the time to see him.

This fruitless existence began to erode his self- esteem. He began to believe that the Jews in New York were worse than the Jew-Killers in Romania.

At times he would regret his coming to America.

Going back to Romania to face the Jew-Killers seemed like the wise thing to do.

He finally accepted the fact that he would never again be anything resembling the man he had been in Iasi. He accepted whatever little job he could get.

They were too few and far between to become stepping stones to something important. This leader of leaders had spent every bit of strength he had in this battle, but, where many others strode right past him and into successful careers, he faced one failure after the other.

Three years after his triumphant arrival in America, he suffered a fatal heart attack. There was not even a notice in any paper that this once grand man had passed away.

All his family suffered from losing Asser. Schmuel, the last son born in Iasi, bore it harder than anyone else in the family. He firmly believed that America was the killer.

Yettie, Asser's adoring wife, rose to the occasion far faster than anyone else.

She knew that her job was to see to it that her children did not suffer too badly from the loss of their father. She silently bore her grief so that the children would see her as a strong widow who was there for everything and anything that buoyed the remainder of her family.

Her message to her children, spoken in the sternest of the Romanian tongue, contained but one thought.

"Your Poppa brought us here and saved our life. Now we must make it the way he intended it to be."

Chapter Twelve

Duvid Pascal was perpetually confused by this crazy country that he once loved. His Iasi was now a place to stay hidden in. He even delivered his milk earlier, and if some of his customers just accepted the milk but never paid for them, one just accepted that.

How could he chance the ire of the non-payer who in return might cite the Pascal's for some hideous sin that would result in dire punishment for these lowly Jews?

His family constantly prayed for the day they would leave for Paris. Instead, without complaint, they endured the pitiful agonies Iasi laid upon them.

It seemed like years, but actually six months elapsed before they received a dry note from a Iasi official, who had been paid off by Asser while he was still in Iasi, advising them that they were free to travel to wherever they cared to go.

Three days later they left for Paris.

The evening of their arrival in Paris they were met at the train station by the Poznik family, old friends from Iasi, who arrived there with their prized possessions, a tired old horse and a beaten cart. It was a cramped but joyous trip through the streets of Paris.

Yiddish and Romanian words filled the air. It was a unique delight for their friends to speak in their native tongues though the Pozniks managed to get in some French words to show how advanced they were in this new world.

There were few people on the streets that night, but Paris seemed aglow with light.

"Before I take you home you must see the latest marvel of Paris. It is only three years old but our Eiffel Tower is already famed throughout the world."

The Pascals were more than tired, half asleep and frightened by the size of everything around them. The only city they knew was Iasi which was less than a small village as contrasted to this enormously overwhelming metropolis called Paris. But, as exhausted as they were, they were open to anything their hosts suggested.

They were what seemed like miles from this Eiffel thing when they began to glimpse something burning in the sky. Finally they could see a structure rearing before them, and then they were at the base of the most amazing tower they had ever seen.

It awed them, and at the same time frightened them. How could all that metal stay up and not come crashing down upon them? They were beyond awed.

Of more accord was the fact that Poznik had arranged for his fellow ex-Romanian, now Monsieur Pascal, to get a tiny apartment to live in and, of yet greater importance, a job in a Jewish bakery.

There was little pay involved in the job, as all he had to do was to come to the store just before it opened and sweep it clean. But Duvid treasured each Sunday morning when he handed those few francs he had earned to Sarah.

The Pascals were ill-prepared to face living in Paris.

Though he received little salary, the family's expenditures were minimal. Their ability to save francs began to build daily and their dreams of a voyage to America took on a more realistic air.

Life in Paris was beyond complicated. It did not take long for Paris to reveal itself as far from the freedom loving, prejudice-free Paris they had dreamed of.

The easiest part was to find Romanian Jews who formed the bulk of their social life. The more trying was to find non-Jewish French people who accepted them.

It devastated them to find that the Jews in Paris were subject to much the same loathing they had received from the non-Jewish residents of Iasi.

The major difference was the much higher degree of bodily harm one faced in Iasi than in Paris. The Pascals were left with little to smile about, except for the fact that Molly was safe in America.

Each day was started with a prayer that soon their departure time would arrive.

The letters they received from America read as if they were words from the Talmud, stating the real problems they would face on the trip to America.

Essentially, the letters detailed that being in steerage is like buying into hell.

Possibly of greater danger were the imaginary thoughts they would subject themselves to as they awaited that much desired trip.

Chapter Thirteen

"I write the following to ready you for what you will soon be facing. Most importantly, you must be steadfast in your knowledge that no matter what you may have to suffer, your arrival here will make every pain forgettable as you rejoice with the glory of living in this country.

We started our trip not expecting the tortuous days that awaited us. We pray it does not beset you as it beset us."

The letter then detailed such mundane subjects as the smell that would creep up on them and worsen each day. How that odor would intensify with every second that passed. That you may fall asleep but you will soon awaken as if every inch of your body were covered with filth.

"Today, I am sending you two short letters. You won't be able to read the first one for it is written in English. I send it to you so that you will be pleased at how quickly I am becoming a richticka American.

The second letter is identical to the first but, as you can see, it is written in Yiddish so you can understand what I am saying.

Please start learning English. If I can learn this crazy language, so can you. Believe me, it will make life much easier for you when you get here. I will be so proud of my family that speaks three languages.

There is a saying here which shouts out 'Stand up on your two feet and let the world know that you are every bit as valuable as they are.' Here's to being as good as or better than anyone else in this wild land.

Kisses and hugs from a daughter who sorely misses you."

Molly

Chapter Fourteen

In her letters to her sister Sarah, Yettie added a further alert about giving any credence to the rumors that are spread by maddened fellow travelers. In the plainest of words, she warned them of gossipers and worriers who delighted in spreading rumors of the horrors awaiting them.

Molly, on the other hand would always add the most personal and comforting of thoughts.

"I miss you, Mama, and you, Papa. I even miss those two boys who claim to be my brothers. I love you all so very much. However, soon we will be together again, and I will smother you with kisses.

I must be very strong, for nothing we have gone through has bothered me at all. I eat, I sleep, I dream good dreams, and I haven't stopped smiling at all. Of course, much of my good thoughts come because the Sinvalorvitz family treats me as if I were a special gift to them.

Yes, each clear day of our trip brought out dozens of us racing to the open deck above. It was the only way to fight off the stench that covered us below decks. An additional pleasure came with many of our fellow travelers bringing musical instruments along with them on every trip to the deck. The resultant singing and dancing brought with it a sense of joy and freedom."

She then told the wonderful tale of Schmuel discovering a very elderly man who had placed his cot next to Schmuel's. It seemed like he did nothing but read all day from a worn Sefer Torah.

"Schmuel, as ever the explorer, talked with the man and, wonder of wonders, the man turned out to be a Rabbi. It took Schmuel little time to tell the man that he was of Bar Mitzvah age and then plead with his newly found Rabbi to lead him through the Bar Mitzvah rites. They immediately jumped into work preparing for the big event. Word quickly spread that a Bar Mitzvah would soon be taking place."

It was just three days after his thirteenth birthday that Schmuel was cheered by all as he officially was declared a man.

Some weeks later, Molly wrote her parents telling them how Schmuel had taken the very long and overly Talmudic speech that the Rabbi had written and had torn it up.

"Every word in the speech that Schmuel spoke, in particular the brevity of it, was from the pen of 'The Quiet One.'

The day before he was to give the speech he told me he was going to deliver it in the best English and Yiddish that he had. He said that the speech was about the future, and English was going to be very important in our future.

He very slowly delivered every word of that speech. It was as if he was making up the words as he went along. Here is that speech:

'Ich denken dir far du bencht mir mit deiner forshlen. Ich kenisht tankein miner vonderful Rebbe ginik.

Ich vil oichit redin in English abur nisht azoi goot und a bissel Yiddish.

I do so, because English is our future, and we have to speak their language now.

My Momma and Poppa gave me the best gift I could ask for and that is taking us to America. I hope everyone here shares a beautiful life there. I know you are as excited about vat avaits us as I am.

Together ve vil make our new homeland even a besser stadt filled with besser people. Ve should all swear to be the best people in America.

Ve are going to make America zer proud of this new group of refugees.

I love you. I bless you. I thank you.'

As soon as Schmuel sat down a roar of approval broke forth. The entire audience seemed to jump to its feet as one and screamed their approval for many, many minutes.

I must confess that I stole up to him and gave him the biggest of kisses on his right cheek. He later told me that he did not wash that part of his face for the remainder of the trip."

Molly

Chapter Fifteen

The Pascal most affected by the stay in Paris was Duvid. He, above all, wanted to be in America, attacking all of the problems there and making it the best place in the world. The delay in waging that war was infuriating.

The man who in Iasi showed little interest in money had become obsessed by the need for francs. His dream of being financially ready for America became an obsession.

The job that the Pozniks had obtained for Duvid paid very little. He soon added a job at a nearby butcher store. It required his getting to the store at five A.M. each morning, so that all the slicing of the meat would be done by early morning.

Three hours later, he was at the bakery.

He was particularly joyful when he added yet a third job. A very elderly couple needed constant care from ten in the morning to seven at night.

It never bothered Duvid that he had but little time for himself or his family. Little sleep and running from job to job slowly wore him down. He was constantly tired. He never acknowledged the fact that minor illnesses became part of his life.

He was far from the Duvid he had always been. A strong cough became his constant companion and soon it was accompanied with heavy phlegm being ejected after each cough.

No matter the calls from Sarah that he go see a doctor; no matter the fact that he was obviously losing weight -- he never acknowledged the fact that minor illnesses became part of his life.

His oft repeated response was, 'When we get to America all will be well.'

Chapter Sixteen

You should know that most new refugees in America needed to be close to where their friends from the old country had settled in this new land. Having fellow countrymen around them provided a feeling of comfort and assurance that was much needed in this chaos called New York.

One lovely Sunday in June, little Idala, Molly's dearest friend in Iasi, who had arrived at least six months before the Sinvalorvitz family, decided that Molly must have made it to New York by now.

She called out to her mother that she was going to visit Molly. That brought forth a veritable screech from her mother.

"Oy Vey is mir. Ich hub fahgosen. Ven de redst Molly's muter gib a gries fin meir."

Idala had but turned three corners when there she was, her Molly. From a half a block away the two girls espied one another and within seconds they hugged and kissed and screamed at one another. It was as if they had not missed a day together.

Do you want to find a friend who is Russian? Go to my old neighborhood, Brighton Beach, and within an hour or two you will find a handful of friends.

If you are interested in Germans, just pop off to Yorkville in East Manhattan. Do I need to tell you about China town or where Italians gather or folks of Greek heritage or the myriad number of other areas that shout out 'Hey here we are. We've been waiting for you?'

Oh, you live on the west coast of the U.S. of A. and you are looking for Jews from Poland, go to Santa Monica just before it becomes Venice.

Wherever you come from, you will find a special someone who will greet you excitingly, for they have been waiting for you to make your appearance for some time now.

That certainly was the case for Idala and Molly. After one glance they were off doing what they always did when they were together. For the next three hours they yentered away.

Per usual, Idala was the chief yenterer.

'You know ven ve ver livink in Iasi, I vas alvays kinish from dir. You alvays ver zer scheina, and I vas meis as a poison could be. Today, you are scheiner den ever, I am still a meiskite, but just looking at deiner punam makes me feel poifect all over.'

Big sentences demand equally big translations.

'You know when we were living in Iasi, I always was jealous of you. You were so pretty and I was so ugly. Today you are still pretty, and I am still as ugly as possible.'

Idala immediately turned to tales of her New York boyfriends which set Molly off into another torrent of laughter. Of course, most of her stories were pure fiction.

First off, she was four feet ten inches when she stretched out as far as possible. Or, as my Mother used to say, while holding her arm at waist level, 'She vas dis big all over.'

So she was beyond short in height, but in any other measurement, she was the tallest of the tall.

Her mouth was six foot three and her passion for singing, with a screechy voice that could peel the skin from your body, was beyond belief. This unreal woman never stopped laughing nor singing old Yiddish songs.

To hear her sing Ba Mir Bist du Schain was to open your heart to a world of lovers.

Her favorite conversation piece was the stories she concocted. More often than not they would concern the many boyfriends she was constantly turning down. The most marvelous thing about her was that once you got to know her, you had to love her.

There was no doubt but that Idala, just as she was in Iasi, still claimed title to being the biggest fabricator in all of New York. All delighted in these fictional romances.

In other words, Idala accepted what God had laid out for her and turned her life into a barrel of fun for all who loved her.

Now with her dearest friend at her side, pairing up with Sophie and Schmuel, it was easy for Molly to enjoy her new world.

Chapter Seventeen

The following month a letter was received by the Sinvalorvitz family. The message was printed in capital letters and, wonder of wonders, in perfect English. It is what we were all praying to hear. It simply said.

'WE HAVE OUR PERMISSION TO LEAVE PARIS. WE ARE SCHEDULED TO GO TO DOVER IN ABOUT TWO WEEKS.

THEN WE HAVE JUST ONE WARNING FOR YOU.

WATCH OUT AMERICA. SOME CRAZY FOLK FROM ROMANIA ARE FINALLY ON THEIR WAY TO SEE YOU!'

Molly's reaction to same note combined insane laughter and a heart filled with the essence of joy.

Chapter Eighteen

The trip to Dover for the Pascals was leisurely, as compared to the hell they received the moment they boarded the tramp steamer that would carry them to America.

Molly's two brothers, seven year old Chiam and five year old Schlmo, who both refused to respond to any name but those two nicknames, were tortured by the restrictions placed upon them.

The lack of toilet facilities was second to the tasteless food that was daily forced upon them. The boys adjusted to the taste and soon began crying for how little of it they were given.

Most of the trip was one indignity suffered after the other. It was far from a pleasant time.

The one joy they experienced was almost identical to what Molly had written about.

Moments of musical pleasures would occur when most of their below-deck companions rushed up to the first open deck.

Many would be carrying a musical instrument and with their arrival came a feast of singing and dancing, As much pleasure as that music brought them, it was nothing as compared to the real joy that filled their hearts when a shout came up that land could be seen not too far ahead. It took two days to reach that land.

Arriving at the Ellis Island dock put non-stop smiles on their collective faces.

The first and second class passengers were swiftly and courteously welcomed into this haven called America.

Oh yes, some of the more esteemed arrivals went through a mere fifteen minute chat before debarking from the boat.

The Pascals and their fellow steerage mates suffered a rather different approach. They were all subjected to treatment that was, at its best, uncomfortable.

For the Pascals they delighted in the knowledge that within moments they would be walking down the gangplank and into the arms of their Molly. That thought made every hardship feel like a gentle wind brushing their faces.

What first awaited them was a building that had been in use for only five years. It was sparklingly clean and most welcoming. One was filled with a joy as the promised dream of America was about to come to them.

The Pascals cried a bit, laughed a bit and shouted out their joy.

The people greeting them were most concerned with efficiency and speed. They were briskly ushered off the boat and onto a long line where their official papers were closely examined.

Both the officials and the émigrés were anxious to be done with this formality. A few people were sent to a different room and never seen again.

The next stop brought them to a horde of doctors attacking them with stethoscopes at the ready.

The Pascals advanced boldly, knowing that each passing moment brought them closer to Molly.

Sarah Pascal zipped through her 'six second' medical examination and the boys received equal treatment.

It was different for Duvid Pascal.

Chapter Nineteen

First one doctor examined him, then another doctor was called to look at him. These two concentrated solely on his eyes. A third doctor focused on the chest area. Much discussion continued between the three.

Duvid was ushered to a different room, where several other doctors continued a now intense examination.

Sarah, Mendel and Benjamin, huddled outside the room. Not being told anything that was going on with Duvid left them with mixed emotions. Their anxiety level grew with each passing moment.

Duvid was greeted by a smiling doctor who introduced himself as just a guy named Bernie Roth and that he spoke perfect Yiddish and somewhat faulty Romanian. That man shook Duvid's hand as he told him not to worry.

Every word the doctor spoke was translated into Romanian or Yiddish.

"You do have a problem with your eyes. It has not been known about for very long and we still do not know much about it. All we know is that it is a genetic disease which can be passed down from one generation to another or skip many generations, only to reemerge after many have lived without it. It is called retinitis pigmentosa."

Duvid started out of his chair but the doctor took his shoulder and gently pushed him down.

"Please hear me out. There is good news as well. Though there is a chance that it may affect your children and it cannot be cured, that needn't change anything about your coming into America.

"So vat's mit mine oigen?"

"We know so little about the disease that I cannot give you an intelligent answer."

"But vot you say about America is true?"

"Absolutely true."

"Den don't vorry. Ich bin a starker. Ven der is somting wrong mit me ve vil talk on it and I vil get gizint."

"But we have more to say that is of greater impact. So that we are certain you fully understand what we are saying would you rather speak in Yiddish or English?"

Very proudly Duvid told them that for two years now he had been studying English, so they could use any language they wanted to. Trying to lighten what was to come, he suggested that it would be better if they chose the language they were more at ease with.

"Or better still, you speak in Yiddish, and I'll speak in English. Den ve vill bot have tsouris with farstaiyin vat the other is saying."

"That sounds good to me. But let's both try English, and if we have something important to say, we can always switch to Yiddish. I haven't used my Yiddish in sometime but if that is okay with you, it is fine with me."

Thus both the doctor and the patient found a way to communicate. Each seemed to care for the other. It slowed their pace but kept the smile on their faces.

"What I have to say is not easy. Please let me tell you what we have discovered, and then I will answer any questions you might have."

The two men looked at one another. Finally, the doctor started explaining that he had some very difficult things to say.

"Sir, you have two diseases. This other disease you have faced is very serious. It brings with it many more fearful problems we must face."

Duvid, with a touch of bitterness in his voice, replied that he was never sick. He was ready to attack the world, and eager to show what he could do in this land of freedom.

"I vil vin no matter vat ever it is."

In Yiddish the doctor told Duvid, with a quiver in his voice, that the problem facing them was not the vision problem.

"It is a disease called tuberculosis and it is a killer."

"I haven't heard from dat. Vat does it mean?"

He stood tall facing the doctors. His fists were clenched and his eyes were blazing. It was as if two adversaries were facing one another, with neither side willing to concede a thing.

Doctor Roth asked Duvid to quietly hear him out.

"Believe me when I tell you I am on your side. When one tries to enter this country you must pass some important tests. Here there is a law that states, if you have a disease that can be spread to others in our country, say one akin to tuberculosis it is...."

He then found it difficult to finish the sentence.

One of the other doctors took over. In English he blurted out, "What Dr. Roth is trying to say is that no one with that malady is allowed to enter our land."

Roth repeated what had been said, but in Yiddish softly adding, "Unfortunately. You do have such a disease."

Duvid felt as if someone had split his heart with an axe. He fell back into his chair. His open hands clutched his knees and he began to shake all over.

Unspoken words stabbed at him as his eyes pleaded with the men surrounding him.

In a frenzy the tortured man finally screeched out, "You are mishiga. I see gons git, and I have noting dat is umrecht mit me.

I am like a strong cha'ya. I am almost thirty-two, and I have never been sick. You have made a bad, bad greiz. Give me some other tests."

"Mr. Pascal, yet another specialist is on his way what he sees will determine how we proceed. Doctor Martin is famed for his work on tuberculosis. The examinations he will give you are noted for their thoroughness and accuracy."

Chapter Twenty

What seemed like hours and hours passed away but, in reality, only a bit over thirty minutes had elapsed before Doctor Martin rushed in.

A few words passed between the doctors, as Martin immediately began the examination by asking Duvid question after question.

Duvid's answers went to Dr. Martin in English. Mostly they dealt with how their patient saw things and the gravity of that problem.

Numerous tests, none of which involved the eyes, were next performed. Each test seemed to lead to more complex tests. He was asked many questions about his coughing and sneezing. His phlegm was taken away for further examination and later included in the heated discussions between the doctors.

Many more difficult questions were asked of Duvid who lied as best as he could to those queries. The answers did not fool any of the doctors.

A brief conversation was held between all the doctors. It rapidly expanded in intensity and finally a decision was reached. Frowns on their faces were less than good news for Duvid. His almost constant coughing was also no aid for him.

After a lengthy discussion, they turned back to Duvid. Doctors Roth and Martin had been almost combatants in the discussion.

"Ich bin a gitten Yid. Luz mir red'n Yiddish."

Roth then rattled off his being born in Poland and coming to the states when he was three years old. He added that he grew up speaking Yiddish and still considered it to be his native tongue.

The smile left his face as he told Duvid that what he had to say was not easy to say, but say it he must.

"Let me tell you all, and then I will answer any questions you might have."

He then paused to make certain that his words were understood by Duvid.

"Let me begin by repeating that you have two physical problems. The first one is not dangerous to you and is not contagious. You have probably had the one we have spoken of since your teen years."

As the serious words came out every muscle in Duvid's body stiffened as tense as could be. "It is called retinitis pigmentosa. It is a disease of the eyes. People can adjust to it and, therefore, think they have no problems with their vision. However, they all will go blind by their early thirties."

Duvid jumped out of his chair and shouted, "Wrong. You are wrong there must be some mistake. Ich zein allless."

"We equally believe what you say about your ability to see quite well now. Hopefully, you will have good eyesight for many years. But, in the not too distant future, you will start losing your good vision."

And then the doctor added, "Believe me, we are certain you do have retinitis pigmentosa. You will go blind."

Now, really shouting, Duvid disagreed.

"Vat are you talking from. Ich zay gons git. Ich lazen. Mitout brillin."

This time Roth gently folded Duvid's hands into his own.

In the softest of tones said, "Please, listen to me. All who suffer this disease think they have no problems with their vision. However, they all will go blind by their early thirties."

Duvid jumped out of his chair shouting "Umrecht iz Umre iz Umrecht. You are wrong ich zein allless."

"Please listen to me. We are not worried about your vision. In no way will it affect your being welcomed to New York."

Duvid relaxed just a bit.

Roth again took the lead.

"What does concern us is that you also have an illness called tuberculosis. If you are in fact a carrier of the disease we have very serious matters to discuss.

He let Duvid digest the words.

"You may have noticed that each of us have donned face masks. We do that so as to protect ourselves from catching that disease."

Duvid just stared at the speaker. He did not volunteer any information. Certainly not a word about how he had been feeling for some time now.

"I think it is best that I now bring in your wife and tell both of you what I must."

With that an aid brought in Sarah. The boys were ushered into a corner of the room that held a myriad of toys.

"Dear Mrs. Pascal. Today your husband is a very healthy man. He could live for a very long time. He has one disease that can cause him severe problems but he can survive that battle."

In response, she clung closer to her Duvid but did not utter a word.

"That disease will affect his eyes, and though he sees almost perfectly now, he will in time go blind. It is a disease that is common amongst Ashkenazi Jews. There is a chance that each of your sons may get that disease as well."

Sarah merely clung closer to Duvid but still did not open her mouth.

"More importantly, your husband is a carrier of a very infectious and dangerous disease. It is called tuberculosis, and it can affect the lungs or the kidneys or the brains with equal ferocity. All we know about tuberculosis is that it is a killer."

At this point Duvid had almost disappeared in his chair.

"Our almost grievous concern is that we know for certain it is highly communicable. Little is known about the disease other than certain visual elements that warn us of someone who might be bearing the disease. Your husband possesses most of these signs."

Again another even longer pause before the doctor spoke again.

"There is no doubt that he has this dire disease. What I tell you of is merely to prepare you for what lies ahead. Some important decisions must be made."

Sarah clung even tighter to Duvid who could do nothing but gently smooth her hair.

Dr. Roth muttered, "Being a carrier of that disease will prevent your husband from getting admission into this country."

A scream flew from Sarah's mouth. The words were indistinguishable but slowly all heard her faint plea.

"Uber mine my tuchta lives here? What do I do about my Molly?"

Not another word came forth. The boys, consumed with a new game they had just learned, continued unaware of anything but the game.

Their parents, awash with tears, were locked in a world of gruesome pain.

Dr. Roth softly suggested that they pray that one day a cure would be discovered and the gates of America would be open for them.

"You have only one decision to make. You, Mrs. Pascal, and the boys can remain in America, but your husband must be returned to whence you came from."

Sarah, looking up, softly whispered in her best English.

"Those are the most stupid words I have ever heard. Put us back on that boat. We are a family not four strangers."

Chapter Twenty-One

Outside on the street Molly, Sophie and Sam were befuddled by the number of people emerging from the boat, but there was no sign of the Pascals. After some time, the crowds had dwindled down to where there were only five groups still waiting at the gate.

At last a man with a very sour face approached the few dozen very nervous people.

"Listen up. The names I am about to read are of those families that have a variety of diseases. By law, that prevents them, at this time, from entering our country. They will be shipped back to their point of departure. Should I call out the names of the folks you are interested in please step forward, and I will give you a more detailed report."

One half hour later the name Pascal was called. The worst words they could ever expect to hear were slowly spelled out to them.

"We are very sorry, but Mr. Pascal will not be able to enter our country.

Schmuel, who somehow maintained control, raised his hand as if he were in school and asked, "What about Mrs. Pascal and the two boys?"

"They have all opted to return to Paris with Mr. Pascal."

Molly was stricken with fear. She slowly crawled to her aunt Yettie and collapsed into her arms. Her body froze with the thought that she would never again see and touch her mother Sarah, kiss her father Duvid and delight in her two little brothers, Mendel and Benjamin.

It was as if God had singled out this nice family and made them pay for all the horrors that coursed through this cruel world.

Chapter Twenty-Two

Molly died a thousand deaths each day.

She swore that she would be off to Paris as soon as she could, but got no support from either side of the ocean for that venture.

No matter that she kept screaming that she belonged in Paris with her family. Neither father nor mother would allow her to think of such a stupid move.

Each of the almost daily letters she sent off to Paris was started with the same request.

"Please, please let me come to Paris. Ich staub avec a bisell allla tug mit mine benken dir."

It would not take too long for her to realize that she would never receive a positive reply.

When Molly was assaulted with the current situation, she was beyond knowing how to cope with the terror of what her real life was about to become. How could she live without a mother, a father and those two delicious brothers of hers?

Letters flowed in a steady barrage from New York to Paris. At first they were fiery in their desire to fight the stupidity of the laws formulated by the American government.

Then weeks would pass by without a letter from either side of the ocean. Next it was months that drifted away as the letters became less frequent and far less fierce.

Just living their separate lives became the dominant factor in each of their lives.

The pain in Molly's heart lingered for many years, but, bit by bit, the daily battle of living in the Lower East side took precedence over the loss of so many people who meant so much to her.

Chapter Twenty-Three

As time continued without any change for Molly, the pain lingered on, as outwardly, she seemed to have accepted what her life must be.

Inwardly, she was living the life of a dead person. Each morning she arose from an almost sleepless night with tears pouring down her pot-marked face. The tears rarely stopped. Her self-hatred plagued her daily.

She would relate those feelings only to Schmuel who never did anything but listen quietly to her sad words.

He knew that there were no words that could change the situation, but having somebody to release her inner thoughts to allowed her freedom from the agony of it all.

Her pretty face…her lovely laugh... her wondrous smile… the sparkle in her eyes… the lilt in her voice …each day all vanished further away to be replaced by a death-like approach to living.

This sweet young lady pondered suicide as the only real answer to her dreadful life. Schmuel became Molly's constant confidant. His mission was simple enough. He must find the words that would dry her tears and open her heart wide enough to accept a taste of happiness and, in doing so, replace the sordid thoughts that every day besieged her.

He had two allies in this battle.

One was his mother, Yettie, who had all but forsaken her children and replaced them with Molly as her pet need.

The other was Idala who used every device she knew to get an occasional smile to grace Molly's face.

Though he knew it would be a tragic mistake, Schmuel volunteered to be at Molly's side when she was ready to leave for Paris and make that city their home.

She loved him more for that offer but knew she could not accept it. How could she drag him down a path that could only be destructive? How could she take this man that she always loved and destroy his hopes forever?

The worst horror was that deep down she knew that she really wanted to stay in her new land.

Chapter Twenty-Four

One evening Schmuel and Molly took off on a walk through their bustling neighborhood. For the longest time, there was not a word exchanged between them, and then he stopped and turned towards her.

As usual, when important matters were to be discussed, the words were spoken in the Romanian tongue. For your convenience, I have translated their entire conversation.

"Molly, you are right. I think you should go to Paris, and I will go there with you. First you will get a job here, and between us, it shouldn't take more than a few years to get the money we will need."

"Would you do something like that just for me?"

"Of course not! I got to thinking that most American girls do not appreciate what a fine catch I am. So I'll go to Paris where the women are beautiful and they appreciate a handsome man. But don't worry. We can still be friends."

"Do you know that you are crazy?"

"You don't like that idea? Well my other idea for going to Paris is that I have heard that they are having trouble cleaning The Eiffel Tower, and I think I know how to do that. The only problem I could have with that job is that I don't like anything that is tall. Do you think they would let me just work on the first few floors?"

She was about ready to hit him when he stopped her by saying, "There is one other idea I have that I hope you will agree with."

"Schmuel, I've heard enough jokes. Can't we just walk a bit without your bringing up some stupid nonsense?"

"First, I tell this other great idea of mine, and then we will both shut up. I have decided that you and I are going to get married, and I don't think my family need to come to our wedding ceremony in Paris."

It took many moments before she could reply to those words. Her tears joined in equal proportions with her laughter as she hit back with "How do you know I am going to say 'yes' to that proposal?"

"That is simple. I know you hate funerals almost as much as you don't understand other religions, and if you turn me down, I will either commit suicide or become a Catholic Priest."

With that he fell to his knees and with the saddest look she had ever seen said, "I have wanted to marry you since the first time I saw you. Please don't disappoint the whole world by saying 'no' to me."

It was typical Schmuel. If you can't get them to agree with you by being serious try again, but this time with humor.

"Schmuel. thank you for being so crazy, and please don't stop. You are the only one who keeps me alive."

"Do you know how hard it is for me to get into this begging position? Please, I am serious. Would you marry me?"

Molly bent down on her knees and the two joined hands.

"Sam or Schmuel or whoever it is that you are, I would never marry anyone but you."

At this very moment a group of Chasidic men walked by two young people kneeling on the pavement. One was crying and one was laughing.

The leader loudly expressed his opinion about what was going on. "Ich kenist farsteinin da Americanishas menschen. Kushen of un gas…a shanda."

And the group swiftly and righteously sped past the two happiest people in the world.

Schmuel shouted after them in Yiddish that he and Molly were not crazy. That they were Jewish and that they were kissing because they soon would be married.

The Chasids never heard a word of his outburst but wandered off discussing how mishiga kinda are these days.

By the time Schmuel and Molly reached the age of fifteen and thirteen, all knew that they would soon be married. A bit before her sixteenth birthday, the ceremony sanctifying their love was performed.

I would gladly describe that event to you but for the life of me I couldn't get out a word from either Momma or Poppa other than Momma's saying it was a very nice affair.

Chapter Twenty-Five

Idala, was the first in the world to know that Molly and Schmuel would be married when he was eighteen and she was sixteen.

During the weeks that followed, at least with Molly, Schmuel lost the title of 'The Quiet One.' He found he could not stop taking about how lucky he and Molly were and blessing God for bringing them such a great mitzah.

Ida greeted this news with the perfect retort.

"You vant I should tell you someting? I knew dat ven I vuz four years olt."

After hearing this news, Yetti wrote a letter to her sister Sarah telling her that those two crazy children, her Schmuel and Sarah's Molly, had made the decision to get married.

Her final words in the letter were, "Poisonaly I don't know vat has took dem so long to make up der minds. Molly told me that she had already sent that news to you, but I also vanted you to know how happy I am about it."

Only Sophie brought negative thoughts to the happiness that spread throughout the family.

"Die bist a mischigana. You need him like you need a hole in der head."

"Vy vould you say such a ting? He is your brother, and he loves you, but you never even talk mit him? Do you know that he is the sweetest, kindest, best man in the vorld? Also he is the best tanser!"

Without a doubt Sophie's complaints about Schmuel did not bother him one bit.

"Listen she just wanted to be the first one with a 'Mrs.' in front of her name. Who knows, she may pick up some bum and elope with him, so that she can beat you to the altar.

Sophie presented argument after argument, but it dawned on her that there was nothing that she could say or do that would prevent this marriage.

Instead she set out to snare someone for an earlier wedding.

One night Molly told Sophie that she wished her well and hoped that when she met her man he would set her as tingling with love as Schmuel did to her.

That only increased Sophie's despair on not getting her man soon enough.

In private conversation with Molly, Schmuel noted that he liked how all the brides and grooms in the family were marrying away at a ferocious speed. The only groom he disliked was the man Sophie took.

"Believe me, Molly, he is a good for nothing and Sophie is not going to have a wonderful time mit him. He talks like he knows everyting in der vorld and tinks he is God's gift to women. I don't tink he vil efer stop telling me how many girlfriends he left mit a tsbroachena hartz."

Waiting for the proper time to get married didn't suit Molly or Schmuel and their marriage was signed and sealed within the next six months.

The babies were soon on their way and there were no happier people in the world than a couple named Schmuel and Molly Sinvalorvitz.

Chapter Twenty-Six

Poppa did many things with a passion that was uniquely his own. We had grown accustomed to his constant reading, his betting on the horses, his ever stressing the need for more laughter and his devotion to speaking less and listening more.

But he really threw us when he started getting each of us a gift that we would uniquely enjoy.

With Buddy, it was always a small book written by a famed author. Willie got articles on athletic history. Matty loved receiving chocolate bars, and I always got news of a historical event.

I knew a gift would be coming my way when Poppa would shout out to me, *"Schmendric, kim a hare."*

I remember one day his calling out those words and my racing to him while wondering what great gift he had found for me. I was very disappointed when I saw no package awaiting me.

He told me to take a seat and to listen carefully for he had a verbal gift for me. He then went on at great length telling me a remarkable bit of history.

It seemed in the very earliest days after the founding of New Amsterdam, Peter Stuyvesant, then the Director General of a sliver of land in North America controlled by the Dutch, had denied refuge to some twenty three Sephardic Jews. They had been expelled from Recife, Brazil.

Upon hearing of his actions the Dutch West India Company overruled him and the Jews opened their first settlement in what would later become New York.

Poppa finished his historical lecture rather pompously. *"Aha is der any udder Poppa mit facts like dat?"*

All of us kids knew that Poppa took more joy from his 'gifts' than we did.

His ultimate joy was bestowed on the entire family early in December one year when he, with much excitement, told us of a trip we were about to take to a wonderful hotel in the Catskills.

This was to be the first vacation we had ever taken.

None of us were particularly excited about the trip for it covered the New Year's week and all of us, with the exception of Momma and Poppa, did not want to have anything to do with the Catskills.

For one thing, it was colder in the Catskills than on the Lower East Side, but none of our blather could dissuade Poppa from promoting this trip.

High on his list for going to this particular hotel was that the cost could not be lower.

The owners of this hotel were Heschel and Essie Silverman who had emigrated from Iasi to America some years prior to Momma and Poppa.

While living just outside of Iasi, they had been good friends of Asser and all of the Sinvalorvitz family.

They were owner-farmers. Not an easy chore. Between the difficulties of earning a living from that farm and the almost constant anti-Semitism from fellow farmers, they decided it was time to move to America.

At first their intent was to continue farming in America but they quickly learned that farming in that area was not only far harder, but the cash payoff was even less than what they garnered in Iasi.

It did not take them too long to realize that they had other talents that could prove of far more value than farming.

Essie was famed for her cooking talents -- to be invited to her table was akin to being awarded a prize from God.

Heschel had the astonishing ability to take any Yiddish song and when he sang it, it was like you were in the finest vaudeville house in the world.

The Catskills growing reputation as a favorite vacation spot for New York Jews persuaded the Silvermans that there was a better way to earn a living than by the sweat of their brows. Essie and Heschel decided to pool their talents and convert their farmhouse into a small hotel that offered a three way winner.

They did not have the money to do so, but they did have an acquaintance, named Asser Sinvalorvitz, who was then luxuriating in the wine business and a clothing store that was most successful. A note was sent off to Asser in Iasi asking for a loan.

Without asking how they would repay him, Asser quickly sent off to them the funds they requested.

He knew that with Essie's food and Heschel's vocal skills every émigré from Romania would soon be beating down their doors. He sent the money from Iasi without a care.

Heschel and Essie were born to the task. They almost instantly were in the profit mode. It was small but always positive. Their staff was taught that the only words their guests wanted to hear were 'Yes, of course darlink.' It paid off in happy guests and a far richer staff, Be it summer or winter the all-Jewish visitors knew that a week at the River View was cheaper and offered more for them than a day in London. All the potential visitor wanted was a full stomach and delicious Yiddish entertainment at night.

This was easy for Heschel and Essie to deliver. It didn't hurt that the cost for a visit there was very inexpensive. This was particularly shown in the bill offered to their fellow countrymen.

Poppa very carefully explained how he had chosen this particular hotel. High on his list was the very little amount of money it would cost us to do so.

Obviously the cost transformed us into devoted fans of the River View Hotel.

Chapter Twenty-Seven

We were soon bound for the River View Hotel and a week in the Catskills.

We arrived right on time for an enormous dinner, then a brief stroll through the hotel and the environs.

Early the next morning I woke up staring at our ultra-tiny room. Poppa had managed to get two such rooms.

The first was for Buddy and Willie and the other for himself, Momma, Matty and me. I had the pleasure of sleeping with Poppa.

The rooms were quite modest in facilities. To say the least we didn't expect to have a toilet available in our room.

I could see Poppa was stretching a bit and his eyes were beginning to open which spurred me to whisper, "Poppa, I have to pee real bad. Where do I go?"

"So vat do you tink der water sink is for?"

From ten words came a world of wisdom.

You can't imagine how delighted I was to see my pee go up in the air and watch same yellow stream fall into the sink. What a treat. I could empty my bladder, but even better, it taught me to sin yet still get away with that 'wee' transgression.

One hour later an even greater thrill was to come to me. Poppa and I were trudging along on a barren frozen road. We had already walked about fifteen minutes and hadn't seen a soul or uttered a word.

Suddenly, my good father cupped both his hands to his ears, raised his head to the sky and let forth as strong a shout as he could with a determined 'Cock a doodle doo.'

I was so proud of my father challenging the world to awaken that soon the two of us were joined in happily cackling 'Cock a Doodles' to the sky.

My delight with Poppa was enhanced yet again.

That night was New Year's Eve at the River View. It was the latest I had been allowed to stay up. To say I was excited is a gross understatement.

Breakfast, and lunch were mere preparations for what was promised to be a dinner worthy of any famed Lord of the Kingdom.

Once dinner was dished out there was no doubt but that every gourmet maven who was there, you should excuse the expression, was in pig heaven.

Even the gefilta fish and Red Horse Radish was far better than what my folks could turn out.

Essie, though she was barely five feet tall, delivered a meal that was beyond belief in both quantity and taste.

We sat down to be served this endless meal, but before I could pick up a fork, Poppa slid his hand over my left calf, squeezed quite hard and whispered in my ear, *"Don't fress too much."*

Momma, seeing I hardly ate anything, comforted me by saying, *"Totala, not to vorry. You have a mishiga Poppa. Eat vat you vant. It von't hurt."*

I managed to fake out both Momma and Poppa by shifting much food from fork to lap to floor, while seemingly furious chomping away with teeth and cheeks and very little food in between.

I finished this coup by telling Momma how great the food was and then getting permission from Poppa to taste the desserts which he happily agreed to.

Poppa never discovered that I ate about seven of the gooiest, tastiest creations ever offered me.

Other than that night, I must confess I was bored out of my mind the entire weekend. There were no other kids at the place and my siblings didn't seem to find any room nor time for me.

Watching the 'the alter cockers' rocking back and forth on the porch as they yentered away was a bore.

I wanted to scream out, "It's rest time. All you must do now is to close your mouths until you are called in for your next banquet meal."

I never did muster the courage to do same.

Chapter Twenty-Eight

Back home Momma intensified her assaults on our local food shops.

Momma had the soul of a man who worshipped accurate financial records. Combine this with a firm belief that every shop keeper was dedicated to stealing from her.

She would go shopping every day from ten in the morning and return to prepare lunch for me. I would race in and a sandwich and a glass of milk would be on the kitchen table waiting for me.

She would be sitting on the opposite end of the table pencil in hand. Her glasses firmly in place on her nose and her head buried in the receipts from each of the stores she had shopped in.

It could well have been tomatoes or eggs or chickens or meat. Whatever.

She would go through the list at least twice to finally determine which, in her words, bastids, had cheated her and then immediately dash out to confront the gonif or gonifs that had stolen from her.

Now it could have been a nickel or a quarter, but she knew the exact price of everything she bought, and no one was going to get away with stealing even a penny from this lady.

I had tried arguing with her about how hard she was working and how little return she was getting.

Once, and I mean just once, I ventured that didn't the man in the store sometimes make a mistake in her favor?

Her response was a quick and fiery.

"De bist a pisher. Vus can you veisen from people who make a living by stealing from poor people like me."

On the rare occasion when she did find some discrepancy, an 'Aha' would explode from her and she would fly out.

She would return not with more money but with extra pieces of whatever they had tried to rob her of. The smile on her face reflected that once again she was the winner.

My mother ruled the roost in our house. She was far from an innocent. She ruled what we ate, what we wore, and, most important of all, where we lived. Mom loved, above all else, to change our living quarters as often as possible.

True to her dictates, these moves were done with our rental costs never going up, the apartment always growing in size and being part of a nicer neighborhood.

I don't believe she ever lost a battle where her family was concerned.

The word Balebusta had to have been created for my mother. It means a feminine boss. As it refers to my Momma its meaning is the dictator, the ruler, the setter of all rules, one not to be contradicted.

But she did it all without ever issuing a harsh word. Her smile drew you to her and you were glad that this woman was yours to keep and cherish.

Now my mother was no ardent super religious Jew but each year for Chanukah and Yom Kippur she would always manage to sneak into our local Temple and enjoy the services.

That's right. She never purchased a ticket since it was simpler to just roll into Temple without same.

When I admonished her about doing such an act, she laughingly looked at me as if I was the world's biggest schmendrik.

"Vat does it matter dat dey let me, a very poor vuman, to daven mit dem for a few hours?"

Momma lived by her own rules. She balanced the money she had against the money the Temple had and decided her manner of going to services was the fair way of doing things.

She and Poppa shared the same view of religion. Both loved being Jewish. The three of us were having a quiet conversation when out of the blue I asked what they thought about being Jewish.

Momma kept nodding away while Poppa took on the answer.

"Dat is zer hard to say. Foist I should tell you that Momma and me love being Jewish. Ve are very proud of vat the Jews have done in the past tousands of years to make dis voild a healthier place, a smarter place, a richer place for many people."

He looked for my response, but as I was about to have a go at him, he held up one finger stopping me from saying anything while he added yet another thought.

"Ve Jews have done many good things even some great tings while the goyim, and I don't mean all of them, have spent their days gihargating the Jews. So, yes, we love being Jewish but do we believe der is a God. No."

He went on to talk of Momma's family living in Paris. At some length and for the first time he went on about his brother poor little Zeldin and the terrible life he had led.

Momma's total agreement was readable from her tear-filled face.

"But vat I said doesn't mean that people who believe in dar God and need dar God are wrong. If it makes life easier and besser for dem, if they are Jewish or vatever, I say 'Tank you God' you are doing a great job for doz people."

Chapter Twenty-Nine

One day Schmuel asked Molly if she would be interested in his getting her a job. She smothered him with kiss after kiss. He almost died with embarrassment but the very next day he put the words into action.

His knowledge of people who had jobs valuable for young girls was small but within a few days he had corralled jobs for both girls in a 'schmatta' factory owned by a client.

One such man, Irving Grossman, owned a small sweat shop. Schmuel asked him if he could be in need of two zear schein madelach who oichit are very good workers?"

Upon hearing of Schmuel's sister and her equally versatile cousin, and the fact that they were quite attractive, he simply replied, "Midout a question. Every day I have to hire more people."

Grossman was not the nicest of people. He was a rather loud mouth braggart who was always talking about the big clothing business he owned. Actually Grossman owned only a small piece of a very small cheap ladies' dress company.

Whether the business was large or small was of no matter, nor of no importance was the ownership of the company. What mattered was that it gave Sophie and Molly the chance to earn some money.

Like every company in the garment trade the words 'sweat shop' was the perfect acronym for this place of work.

Should you not know the meaning of the words 'sweat shop,' you are obviously not from New York.

A sweat shop was one of many companies in the very competitive clothing game that fought each day for their fair share of the 'biz.'

The owners would stoop to any level to keep all expenses as low as feasible, and profit was the only word that mattered.

Thus their workers, be they twelve or forty years of age, were paid close to nothing, as their bosses kept screaming at them to work harder and faster.

Water poured from the these workers in the heat of summer and the frosts of winter cut through the tons of clothing they wore in a vain effort to keep from freezing.

Being desperate for money most of them gladly accepted whatever they were paid and whatever else conditions were.

If the workers were not sweating they were not working hard enough. To ensure the greatest output possible there was always a man screaming at them.

A good deal of the time it was Grossman himself screaming at his all-women employees.

'Vat? You vant I should throw you all out on the street? I promise you that's vats going happen unless you turn out more goods.'

He was accordingly called the 'svitzer.' The man who brings forth sweat.

It only took three days for the cousins to realize what kind of shop they were working in. The only thing that mattered was that soon it would be Saturday -- Pay Day.

They had almost instantly learned to hate the job and its owner.

In turn, he was very pleased to have hired these attractive young girls. He had all sorts of plans for them. None of which was even faintly close to being decent thoughts.

The girls could not have been treated better than on the morning of their first day on the job. Schmuel, of course, escorted them to the job.

"I tell you, Sam, these girls are going to do very vell here. Yes Sir, very vell."

They would learn better before the day was over.

Late that afternoon the girls were in a heated discussion, when they espied their boss heading towards their sewing machines. The conversation ended abruptly.

By watching how he treated the other workers they quickly learned how all who worked there contended with this monster of a man.

His favorite saying was, *'No tawkink. Just voiking.'*

Towards the end of the day, Grossman stopped at Sophie's machine.

"Sophila could you come mit me? I have to get some ultra-fine material out of the backroom and my bad back won't let me get to them."

She followed him into his back office where he told her of some priceless cloth which had fallen down behind the cot that was stretched out in the back of the room.

"Just reach down in da back and you'll see da fabric."

She did as requested, while he said, "Just a little further out." A second later, she felt a hand crawling up her skirt.

He had made a mistake. As the hand touched skin, there was an eruption that burst up from beneath him.

Sophie had jumped up into air, spun around and in the doing of same had landed a smashing kick to his testicles.

He fell moaning to the floor, as Sophie apologized for her accidentally hitting him.

"Oh I am so sorry, Mr. Grossman. I hope I didn't hurt you. I guess you will never again have to bring me back here. May I also suggest that my friend, Molly, has even less control of her flying feet."

He never again touched either girl and they, in turn, produced more work for him than any of the other women in the room.

The only item of importance to either of the girls was the pay check. Though the pay was miserly and the working conditions were beyond dreadful, they never even thought of leaving that sweat shop.

Chapter Thirty

The first encounter with Grossman taught both Sophie and Molly to keep away from him. Being nice to the 'Sweater' meant keeping him as far away from you as possible.

Yes, some of the women would accept not having to work as hard as the others and, in return, received a higher salary for indulging this man in his vile attempts to lure them into his office.

He had been in New York City some twenty years before any of these rifkas had even gotten out of their diapers. Ergo, his English was more advanced than most of the women. He used that as a weapon to heighten the fear factor they lived with.

Only one thing was of import, *KEEP THE JOB*. Lose the job, and there was no purpose in life.

Once again, it was Schmuel who came up with a plan to ease the pain of their crazy boss.

One evening two men stood outside the shop as all the workers were leaving. One was a huge man. Indeed he was a rarity. He was a Yiddish physical instructor.

Molly and Sophie were near the last to race away after work. They were so busy gossiping, they did not even see the two men lurking nearby.

Had they seen the men, it would still be beyond possible for the girls to identify either of them, as each of the men was dressed in the oddest of clothes and were wearing dark masks.

It wasn't a minute or two before the 'sweater' emerged from the shop, arm in arm with his latest favorite female worker.

The two men spotted the 'sweater' and swiftly came to his side. The smaller of the two gently took the young girl's arm and suggested that she leave the scene.

The far bigger chap grabbed the svitzer, lifted him in the air as the 'sweater' screamed in fright. He was then thrown headlong against the brick wall of the building.

A smash to his face quickly quieted his screams.

"Please don't hurt me. You want money? I can give you money."

The smaller man put his mouth to the ear of the svitzer and whispered, "No mina shtuma. Hairsux Tsu."

In near perfect English the larger man gruffly uttered, "Did that hoit you?"

Then the smaller man took charge.

"Listen good! I don't like vat I have been hearing about you, so I tink it vud be good to change vat you is doink upstairs. Mine friend here vanted to break your bones, but I tol him not tonight."

The larger man pressed his knees into the back of the sweater as the other gentleman whispered final instructions into his ear.

"Ve are going to be regular visitors here. That could mean zer bad times for you. If you don't start being a mensch with these ladies. I vood vorry about vat could happen to you. Fahstay?"

The 'sweater' was then lifted higher in the air and was, this time, thrown against the door he had just emerged from.

Schmuel and his huge friend then walked over to where the 'sweater' lay weeping on the ground.

"Let us tell you von more ting. Ven you are the boss upstairs, you vil be a perfect gentleman, and I mean every day. If ve don't hear good tings about you, den ve vil realy break a lot of your bones before ve put you on a ship dat's going back to Europe."

One last kick to the backside of the 'sweater' sent him flying, and the two assailants backed off.

The 'sweater' was flipped over on to his back. He managed to get out a soft, "I'll do anything you say."

In reply, the smaller of the two men said, "It's as easy as can be. Just keep thinking of laughing and being nice and you will do real well."

Those words quietly ended the encounter.

That night Sophie told Schmuel that she and Molly really wanted to thank the two men who had beaten their boss, but those two had flown the scene before any of the women could reach out to them.

They never learned who was to be thanked for that wonderful change, so they simply praised God who had taken a monster and somehow overnight changed him into almost a nice person.

Chapter Thirty-One

Schmuel, who had never lifted a finger against anyone, was disgusted by his use of brute force, but it was the only way that he could come up with something that might protect his Molly.

Each day his brain formulated fresh ideas, and he prayed that the world would love his ideas and put them into daily practice. There was not one thought of violence in any of his plans At the heart of his thinking were two words that motivated all his thoughts, love and laughter. Every time he tried to move from mere words to some form of action, nobody in his world seemed to know or care for what he was trying to express.

Each of the great speeches he would give, his marrying Molly, bringing forth many children, and a means of securing sufficient money to allow them to live well were meant as a path to a better world.

He and Molly on their nightly walk would explore how to expand his thoughts and make them easier to understand.

Molly would encourage him about how well his ideas would be received. But deep down she knew that there was no money available to support such an effort.

Money was the one plague he could never solve. Much as he dreamed otherwise, he too knew that his every day fight for money would be a constant deterrent to his being anything but a humble tailor.

The pay he earned was far from good, but it would keep the family alive.

His dreams about going to school and becoming a teacher, or getting a job with the government which would allow him to help straighten out the problems that faced the poor people of New York, were just that -- dreams.

Despite all, he seemed to still love everyone he knew with but one exception – Sophie and her new husband to be drove Schmuel nearly insane.

Yes, Sophie got her man and she did marry before Molly and Schmuel.

That marriage was due to Sophie's settling for the first man she could pin down. In the years following their respective marriages, my Mom had nothing but good words for her perfect husband, while Sophie never had anything to say about her man.

The best evidence of which marriage was the better came with the years where Molly produced six children, while Sophie yielded only one girl and, many years later, one boy.

But with the wonder of this ever increasing family came the constant need for more money. Under the weight of this financial pressure, Schmuel made an almost disastrous decision. He left his secure job at the tailor shop and opened up his own shop.

But Schmuel was Schmuel, and his very nature prevented him from making the shop a profitable venture. He would try to be fair in what he charged people for his work, but the customers, far too often, did not pay at all or just what they could afford to pay.

Money was the one plague he could never solve. This resulted in failure for the shop.

I heard much about the Great Depression but did not think we were part of it. Everyone we knew lived from paycheck to paycheck and all seemed to be getting along.

For the longest time we remained desperately poor. So much so, that despite my father always claiming to love being a Jew, we never could afford to join a Temple.

But sometimes good follows bad. One of his favorite customers told Schmuel that he knew of a new clothing store that was about to open. A quick meeting was set up, and the result was a job for Schmuel.

The store, Sam Rosenthal & Sons, was located at 129 Park Row which placed him half way between City Hall and Chinatown in Manhattan.

It quickly became quite popular, and it's most favored employee was the head of its tailoring department, Schmuel, who stayed there for the remainder of his working life.

Over forty years.

Chapter Thirty-Two

As the children and the parents on both sides of the Atlantic grew older, the lives in Paris and New York became more and more complex.

Of greatest concern was that Duvid's health grew worse and worse on an almost daily basis.

He was constantly aflame with anger. His ceaseless claim that America had robbed him and his family of their future was repeated time and time again. He hated every American.

His health became worse and worse and soon he spent more time in hospitals than at home.

Three years later, tuberculosis claimed another victim. One would have thought that now there was no 'raison d'être' to restrain this family of Romanian and French descent from adding American to their heritage.

But the rumblings of World War One cut short any thoughts of a renewed effort to once again try to emigrate.

Some thirty nine years later, another killer of mankind, World War Two, ended and its death reignited thoughts of a family relationship. They never went beyond that.

Sarah, old as she was, could not think of leaving the three men she most loved buried and alone somewhere in Paris.

Yettie, in New York, had all but forgotten that she had dear ones living in Paris.

Truth of the matter is that I never heard of having relatives in France until I was in my late teens.

Chapter Thirty-Three

Past activities were history, and neither Momma nor Poppa really were concerned with the past. Momma and Poppa were more alike than I had thought.

Gosh knows, these two cousins were born for one another.

She became the spokes lady of this marriage and the boss of all the children who just about every year or two soon began arriving.

He, ever so quietly, would teach us how to smile and, therefore, gain a life-long appreciation of how to enjoy what is offered to us.

Abie, who was called Buddy by everyone, was the oldest child. We had a special relationship. I was born on February 12th, which happened to be the day of Buddy's Bar Mitzvah. His birthday was February 22nd. Willie was born on October 27th.

This meant three renowned presidents, Abe Lincoln, George Washington and Teddy Roosevelt were honored by a Dieter, a Buddy and a Velvel. It was the only claim to fame that we shared.

Matty was born on November 13th.

Need I say more?

Buddy held a full time job as a salesman in a fine men's clothing store. He had longed to attend college and often would tell me that this dream would soon occur. Of course, such dreams never do occur.

He usually arrived home from work at eight. I would be lying in my small bed in the boy's room thinking about a myriad of things. Indeed, everything but falling asleep.

One night as he entered the room I turned to him and asked him to please tell me what the word money meant.

He shoved a small chair next to my bed, ruffled my head, and started by saying that this was a tough subject, but he would tell me what he thinks.

He then went on at length talking about the value of money and how you needed it for rent and food and clothes and many other things that one needs to have a decent life.

His lectures were always short in speech, but he answered any question I might have. And, of course, I had question after question. I do think the toughest question I ever asked Buddy was when I posed the following thought.

"But doesn't having a lot of money make you more important than someone who is poor?"

"Dieter, there are other things that are even more important than the accumulation of money. You have to learn to treat everybody equally. Just because one man may be richer than another, that doesn't make him any better."

His answer thrilled me and still does, but, obviously, I had hit something important to him, and he continued.

"Yes, money is important. But it is far from the most worthy thing in life. It is more important to know that recognizing other people's worth and needs are equally important. Give equal attention to everyone you are in contact with."

He then went on at great length about how one should dedicate their life to bettering the world. I fell asleep with those words battling away in my head.

No, I did not succeed in fulfilling the thoughts he had given me, but I have tried to be the man he wanted me to be. Unfortunately, I am too weak a soul to deliver what he thought I could be.

Chapter Thirty-Four

Willie, or Velvel, which is what Mamma called him, was an anomaly in our family. He was an athlete. No, he was more than just an athlete. He was outstanding in every sport he played.

No one in the family could figure out how he got those goyish skills.

As a high school freshman, he made the varsity basketball team. As a sophomore, he was a brilliant runner, yet it was baseball that gave him the most acclaim.

More importantly, he gave me, the worst athlete in America, the greatest gift I ever received. He taught me how to box out a bigger man in b-ball.

He taught me how to play a game that to this day I still love.

He was also more than a bit obsessed with the fact that I had been born. I, unwittingly, had knocked him out of the treasured baby of the family spot. He was just two years old when I was born, and he was given a little rocking chair as a toy to compensate for my arrival. Two days later he smashed his head into an iron radiator which required eight large stitches.

I apologize, Willie.

I had nothing to do with that transgression. But I sure did enjoy the benefits that the young one gets.

My sister Mathilda, or dear Mattie as we all called her, was an enigma her entire life. It seemed as if she was born to do battle with everyone throughout her life.

Unfortunately, she was her biggest opponent. I don't believe she had a truly peaceful day in all her life.

Momma, by far her strongest friend, constantly appealed to her three boys to be nicer and more understanding of Matty.

Poppa showed some compassion, but even he was careful in his dealings with his daughter.

Chapter Thirty-Five

From my earliest years, Poppa kept telling me of the wonders of his father, and I so wanted to do the same for my hero but, other than in my eyes, there was no hero flowing from 'Sam the Tailor.'

Poppa did not depict himself as some immortal. Not once did I hear him utter any statement which even resembled a self-flattering remark. He was the humblest of men who, when asked about himself, might say that he was just a tailor who had the good fortune of marrying his Molly, and together they had raised a good family.

In my eyes, he was a very special person. Yet those who didn't really know the man considered him to be nothing more than a quiet and rather dull, though artfully skillful, tailor.

Actually, his greatest efforts were directed towards making people happy.

Nothing about the man shined out other than his amazing ability to measure a man's body, sew a few stitches, and when the owner of said body, be they short or tall, fat or skinny, donned his new suit, he walked out of the store perfectly attired.

That was all the applause Poppa needed.

One early evening I realized something peculiar about my father. Here was a man who had dedicated his life towards humor. Yet he had only disdain for jokes.

Earlier that day a classmate told me a joke that I thought was a howl. I couldn't wait to rush home and tell it to Poppa. Here is the joke.

There once was a Jewish neighborhood in which there was a very successful Jewish Butcher Shop. It had been there for years and earned a very good income for the Butcher.

For whatever reason the neighborhood began to change as the Jews started moving out to be replaced by a large influx of primarily Italian Catholics. So much so, that a small Catholic church was opened.

The head Priest was given credit for the growth of Catholicism in the neighborhood. He was wise, cared much for his Parish, and used any feasible device to enlarge church membership.

Now the butcher was also known as a wise man. He decided he must talk to the Priest to see if such a man might help with his problem.

The Priest was more than willing to meet with the Butcher.

Hearing the problem, the Priest said there was an easy solution to the Butcher's woes.

"Simply become a Catholic. When people hear of your conversion they will flock to your store."

"But how do I do dat?"

"It's easy. You and I go out to our altar and I say to you, 'Once a Jew, Now a Catholic. Once a Jew, now a Catholic. Once a Jew, Now a Catholic.' And that is all it takes."

The Butcher liked that and proceeded with the conversion. Soon word spread of what had occurred, and his business grew rapidly.

One Friday night the Priest decided to check out the new Catholic.

He followed the Butcher from his store to his house, noting that the man was carrying a rather large package.

Peeking into a small window he saw the Butcher tie the package to an overhead chandelier and three times say, 'Once a Chicken, now a Fish, Once a Chicken now a Fish, Once a Chicken now a Fish.'

Now Molly and I were hysterical after my very good rendition of the joke.

Poppa didn't laugh once. With a very sour face he exclaimed "Dat's not funny."

"Poppa, why wasn't it funny?"

"Foist of all it mekes fun of der Priest, and dat is not nice. Secondly, der Butcher stops being Jewish for getting money, and dat is a sin. Worst of all, it asks everyone to laugh at religion and da people who believe in religion. Doz people have enough tsouris without dat."

I never told my father another joke.

Chapter Thirty-Six

By the time Matty was twelve, and I was about to celebrate my sixth birthday, she did me one great favor. She taught me how to tell time and she gave me a dime store alarm clock. I didn't put down the alarm clock for weeks on end.

Of course, I abused that talent by forever offering to tell anyone what the exact time it was at that very moment. For weeks my brothers avoided me, by saying they didn't have to know what time it was.

Matty had one other ability. She knew everything that had ever happened to our family.

I was puzzled about how infrequently Poppa talked, so I asked Matty about all puzzling issues.

Once she launched into a long speech about what a wonderful man Poppa was and how life had terribly harmed him.

"I guess I was about your age when I first heard about Morris and Leah, and the horrid way they died."

I was as puzzled as can be.

"Who were Morris and Leah?"

Mattie immediately jumped into her pain-in-the-butt mode.

"You must be the dumbest kid on earth. Morris was Momma and Poppa's first child, and Leah came one year later."

I stared at my sister, not believing a word she had said. I had never heard those names uttered before.

Hey, I was the baby. Right?

I listened with mouth agape, as Matty cruelly filled me in. She quickly jumped into the morbid details. I still recall how I reacted to the horror of her words.

She first dwelled on Morris being just a bit over two and that he preferred to run than to walk. He was doing just that, racing through Aunt Sophie's apartment.

At one point, he tripped and ran headfirst into the stove. A pot of boiling coffee atop the stove came pouring down on him.

This inflicted serious burns from his head to his feet. Somehow this led to a severe case of pneumonia. Within two weeks of the accident, he was dead.

Momma was beyond grief.

Poppa devoted every minute of every day trying to bring her through that terrible time. He even made her spend her days with him in his little tailoring shop. He told her he needed her there.

It didn't take long for Momma to realize that that was Poppa's way of bringing her back to her real life.

She also knew that she had to return to being a good wife and mother. Leah was her one child, but she was pregnant with her third child.

Matty wasted no time in getting to the Leah tale. First, she pronounced that this death almost led to Poppa's suicide.

One night Leah went to bed crying far more than usual. As but a four year old, there was no way of Leah telling anyone that she was really suffering.

Momma eventually soothed her, and she fell asleep. She screamed out just once that night as she suffered the pain of ruptured appendicitis.

She died the next morning.

With his sweet princess gone, Poppa disappeared into a world that wouldn't allow anyone else to enter.

What was once a happy man became a mute who never talked and never had a smile for anyone.

Poppa had adored everything about his Leah. She had given him solace about losing Morris, but the added demise of the beautiful little girl that he worshipped was far too much for Poppa to handle.

How do loving parents accept the death of their first two children?

Poppa just stopped talking. Instead he crept into a tiny hole where no one could reach him.

Oddly enough, Momma knew she didn't have the luxury to mourn, but rose to the battle of bringing her husband back to life.

Soon she gave birth to Abie, who I thought was my oldest brother.

Abie and Momma awakened my father to the fact that he too had to have a rebirth.

Nevertheless, it took seven years before Momma and Poppa conceived again.

As Matty said, "Yes, I was that child."

She then went through a long talk that compared the beauty and the charm of Leah to her lack of each.

I believe that Matty's words about Leah's beauty carried with it an apparent jealousy which was the core of her self-hatred.

Chapter Thirty-Seven

Four years later, Willie was born, and two years after that, I came along.

I believe that Schmuel and Molly treated my birth as enough was enough. They now thought of themselves as certified New Yorkers and just shut off the birth valve.

What with half a family left in Paris, and two wonderful children stolen from them, Poppa was forever trying to find ways to get even with the world.

He would always come up with strange ideas but his strangest yet came up early one Sunday when he shouted out my name and then Matty's.

The words sounded so plaintive that we both raced to him thinking something dire had happened.

When we reached him he was seated at the kitchen table with a huge smile on his face.

As we approached him he raised his right hand and pointed his forefinger at us.

'De enfer. I have de enfer. Nechta I decided to schrieb a book. It vuz going to be the story of a mensch I know everyting about.'

He looked at each of us looking for our reaction to this zany idea. All he got was two blank stares.

"Foist I vas goink to scribe a book about me, but today I taut, who cares about me? People don't care a ting about such a facockter mensch. So, I taut and taut and came up mit a besser idea. Ve are going to schrieb about vat appened to our famly, mine siesa kinda. You two will put it all in English."

To say the very least, we were stunned. Poppa's enthusiasm overwhelmed us.

By now, you should know how much I love my Poppa. So accept the fact that I knew this venture was, at the least, foolhardy, but because of that love there was no way I would turn down his 'great idea.'

Much talking was done about Poppa's idea, but not one word was ever put down on paper.

Chapter Thirty-Eight

Poppa rarely spoke about his mother. If I asked him about my Grandmother his only response would be, *"Now dat's a voman."*

If I were to ask him about his father, the reply was always the same. *"Der tallest and best fum der best."*

I've often wondered if my grandparents could have been from a different breed of Jews. Nobody talked about them other than to say how wonderful they were. Then again I've never heard of any Jews being tall so I accepted all said about them.

Somehow, I did get to know my paternal grandmother. Very typical of her was the total love she showered on each of her many grandchildren.

At least once a month, we spent a Sunday at her apartment. She spent most of the hours hugging and kissing my sister, brothers and me so strongly, l was worried that this frail little woman might hurt herself.

When she talked to me, it was if there was no one else in the room. Of course the conversation was held entirely in Yiddish but despite that, I was overwhelmed by how bright my Grandma Yettie was.

When we were leaving, she watched us climb down the four flights of stairs throwing good wishes and kisses down upon us. As we came close to leaving the building, I turned to look back up at her, and she shouted down to me, *"Ich ieb dir mine sesa kint."*

The words were almost whispered, so I barely understood the words she was throwing at me. The smile on her voice was as if she had thrown me a thousand kisses.

I ran back up the stairs and grabbed that frail little woman and kissed her over and over again. As I started back down the stairs I turned back to her and said, "Ich libe dir oichud."

It was the last time I saw this woman who meant everything good to me.

Two weeks later she passed away.

I didn't tell anyone in school why I skipped attendance for several days. I was too embarrassed to tell anyone that my grandmother had just died

For many weeks I wondered about death. Who was that nice lady and why did they take her away from me when I needed her so much?

Chapter Thirty-Nine

I had for some time realized that my father rarely opened up to those outside of his immediate family. On the other hand, he never stopped filling us with moments of delicious insanity.

He deftly taught us that laughter, particularly laughter directed at one's self, was the most rewarding activity one could indulge in.

The theme of one of the most valuable lessons of life he taught us was simple enough. The following is his version of common sense.

'You vake up in da morning. Vat you do is run, run not volk, into di toilet. Dis must be dun qvickly since we have six peoples who vant to go to da toilet at the same times. So you run into da toilet and before you do anyting else you look into the mirror over the sink. You take a good look at your pisk and say very loud, Oy Vey iz mir, ich bin zer miece. Den you vil start to laugh and laugh and the rest of your tug will bring you much glik. And you vil always be zer fralach.

He taught us Yiddish merely by including Yiddish in every talk we had. The word most often thrown in was 'fralach.' I assume you should know by now that 'fralach' means happy. I think my father coined that word.

If we dared to say something that implied being grateful to him for being such a great father he would launch into a seemingly vitriolic tirade in the most unfamiliar Yiddish he could muster up.

After much pleading on our part to tell us what the devil he meant by those words he told us that all he had said was *"Making such a hurrah out of his little voids was a waste of luft."*

Chapter Forty

There must be some kind of God that hovered over people like my parents for soon after Leah's demise the following article appeared on the top of page four of the May Ninth, Nineteen Eleven, issue of The New York Times.

I think the miracle of that story saved my father. I present it below.

FIND PERFECT BABY ON THE EAST SIDE

Abraham Sinvalorvitz Scores 1000 Points In University Settlement Contest.

The physicians who have been presiding over the "healthy baby" contest Inaugurated by the University Settlement on the Lower East Side have discovered a boy baby who is physically perfect.

The infant who has obtained a rating of 1,000 points is Abraham Sinvalorvitz, fourteen weeks old. He lives with his parents at 165 Eldridge Street, which is but a few doors from the settlement.

The perfect baby's parents are Rumanian Jews.

His mother, Mollie Sinvalorvitz, a black-eyed, slender woman, took it as a matter of course that her boy should be pronounced an ideal youngster by the physicians who examined him.

Mrs. Sinvalorvitz is 24 years old. She was married when she was 16 years old, and 'Little Abie' is her third child. Their first child was aged three and a half when he died from a severe case of pneumonia.

The article continues at great length about the details of the contest, the scientific methods applied and the fact that little Abraham was the only one to receive a perfect rating.

Dr. MacLean is quoted as saying to the good Mrs. Sinvalorvitz, as he handed her laughing, dark-skinned baby back to his mother, *"I do not know how you did it but, as I now know it, your baby is perfect in every respect."*

The continuation of the article proved his words didn't faze her for a moment.

"I feed my baby whenever he is hungry, and let him sleep whenever he wants to. I have no regular rules except to keep the child in the open air as much as possible and have him sleep near an open window. If he cries, I pay no attention to him unless he seems hungry. I have never given him a drop of medicine or syrup of any kind. I do not believe in them. If Abie wants to yell, I let him do so. It is natural for children to cry."

The reporter writing the article must have been one helluva of an interpreter. Can you imagine my mother uttering all those words and in perfect English? Not a chance.

Matty insisted that Abie was in that contest because Momma hoped it might help bring her Schmuel back to life. Momma was spot on again.

Poppa was overcome with pride and joy. He wouldn't or couldn't stop giving speeches about his wonderful little Abela.

Mamma told me that the joy of Abie's not-to- believe victory lifted Poppa to be able to once again think and talk about his adorable Leah.

Her final words on the matter were, 'Dun tatah hus bekimen a mensch noch a'mol.'

That sentence demands instant translation. "Your father became a man again."

Chapter Forty-One

Poppa believed in laughing one's way through life. God knows, he was aware of the problems everybody faces throughout their life, but in the deepest recesses of his soul, he believed that a life of sadness would overwhelm you if you didn't laugh your troubles away.

He rarely ventured a word on how to achieve all he hoped for us. In return for our adoration, he would give us a knowing smile or two…sometimes a whole sentence about the meaning of life…or even a thought that would help us enjoy everything we did.

In addition to his wisdom, he also had one outstanding feature that always caught your eye. One mere glance at Poppa staring back at you and you were smitten with life-long envy and love.

The reason for this passion was the beyond beautiful and wondrous blue eyes that he sported. No, I am not talking about faint blue eyes. I mean the bluest of blue that captured your attention from the very second he flashed them at you.

His eyes were beyond belief. They reached out to you and, as they did so, you were captured by the love those welcoming eyes expressed.

My sister, the ultra-dramatic Matty, entitled him 'Mr. Gorgeous,' but I just called him 'Poppa' and thanked him for being my Poppa.

Typical of him, he never made mention of being Mr. Gorgeous or anything else that might bring praise his way.

There might have been some blue-eyed Gypsies or some slightly blue eyed Christians in Iasi, but let me assure you, none with eyes as blue as Poppa's.

No one could come up with a legitimate answer to his blue eyes except the jealous ones who claimed it must have been some traveling salesman who spent an evening or two with Poppa's mother.

In reply to someone telling such a fabrication, Poppa made us repeat in Yiddish the following sentence, *"Mir dof hubem grosser kulones ven mir red asoy."*

Those words translate into 'You better have huge balls when you offer such a thought.'

For, he always added, his Mama's reply would inevitably come with a frying pan smashing down on the speaker's head.

Grandma Yettie was not one to play games with.

Dare you cast a shadow on her or her Schmuel that in any way defamed either of them your life would become one long travail.

It wasn't till many years later that he brought up the subject again. We had been talking about the word 'tolerance' and Poppa kept arguing that one being 'tolerant' showed great strength of character while I said it really showed weakness.

"Listen, do you remember ven ve talked about mine blue eyes and mine Mamma?"

I replied that I had never forgotten that talk but what did it have to do with tolerance.

'Voodn't the vord tolerant be a besser vay to have looked at the whole mishigas? Vood it have been so shreklich if she did have done such a ting? Poppa vas still mine Poppa…Momma was still mine Momma. Notink changed in anybody's life and efshur, just efshur, Momma enjoyed herself dat night.'

I had no thought to contradict what he had just said. The only thing I knew for certain was that he had just given me a way to be a much better man.

Chapter Forty-Two

Poppa had one favorite Yiddish saying that covered his most important feeling on the meaning of life. It was crazy in Yiddish and just as mad in English.

'Az mir dof huben kinder aber me kenisht gain kocken vous ken me tien?'

In English it reads, "if you must have children but you can't go to the toilet what can you do?'

He told that to me many, many times before I had the courage to tell him that it did not make any sense in either language and would he explain to me what it meant.

"Vat it means is nutting....just like the vorld. De vorld is filled mit nutting. Mit pipple who are nutting. So you shud laf at de vorld and den you vil be able to injoy life."

Let me demonstrate yet another of his ploys that he used to teach me about laughing.

The Saturday before the start of the Jewish New Year's Holiday, Poppa came home with a special gift for me. He took me into his bedroom saying, "*A* mensch *who is bolt eight yerz olt, shud vear a real suit for dis yontif.'*

With that, he opened the package he was carrying and revealed a marvelous grey woolen three piece suit. Within moments I was draped in the suit that was too big in every direction.

Soon Poppa was making chalk marks over just about every inch of the garment. Of course I was more than aglow with the realization that I was almost a man. Goodbye pants that end at the knee, and hello manhood.

He was just about finished with the marking up when he looked at me and with a very serious tone told me the following.

'Now, ven you put on the pants make sure you push your smendrick to the right side. Never leave it on the left side.'

I looked at him like he was a crazy man.

"Poppa, what difference does it make where it goes?"

"Lissen to me. Von tag you have an axcident and you pee a bissel on the wrong side. Peeple vil see it and laf at you and tink you are not a mensch. That is vy I told you vat to do."

I considered that for quite some time and it still did not make any sense to me.

I turned to Poppa and was about to start an argument with him about the placement he had ordered, but I happened to first look into his face, and I could see his eyes were laughing at me.

His eyes ended this battle as they seemed to be saying just eight words.

'Always lissen, but don't buy evertink you hear.'

These words were followed by a rare but hearty laugh from Poppa.

I learned much from both the words and the laughter.

Chapter Forty-Three

I believed that my Poppa liked me better than any of his other children for it seemed I was always there when he opened up and dazed me with his wit and wisdom.

More likely, it was because I, as the youngest, always stayed close to this man I so loved.

Because of that closeness, I learned much from my Poppa. I was able to adjust to everything a kid faces. I adopted his every word as my philosophy on how to best face this mad earth we live in.

But the one thing that continued to bother me was that crazy name I had been endowed with. I can still hear the kids in school, who in my neighborhood were almost all Jewish, yelling at me "Hey, Dummy, how's your Sinvalorvitz getting along with your Dieter."

The first time I asked Momma about my name was early one Sunday morning.

'You vant to know from your name? Dat is taka a easy ting to tell you.'

And with that, she walked into our little kitchen where she was creating a heeping bowlful of 'Salada di Venita'.

Ah yes. What is 'Salada de Venita'? Well, first of all that is its Romanian name, while it is called 'Potla Jel' in Yiddish and probably had as many other names as there were other tongues spoken in this crazy world. Whatever the name, it is simply the most delicious salad that has ever been created.

This was the mandatory first course that introduced a meal Momma was making for the dozens of our relatives and a mass of other former Romanians that would be eating with us in about five hours.

Without pause, for the hundredth time, she jumped into the exact details of how this delicacy was to be prepared.

"Dis is de only vey to make the best Salada de Venita. All Romanians lof how I make it."

And then, of course, out came all the details of preparing the dish.

'You must toin de egg plant over and over a hot fire fur a gitten five minutes Den you peel da skin avay and den chop it in a vooden shisel.'

"Right Mom, and then you add lots of onions. But what about my....."

She quickly cut me off.

'Foist I put in tomatoes den cucumbers and den, if you have dem, radishes and spritz a bissel salt over it. Den come de best onions you can find and finally soak it mit Italian Olive Oil. You mix everyting togetter, and keep it in da ice box for at least drie hours. Ah, it will be a michaiyo.'

I had the pleasure of cutting her off again.

"Momma, my name, my name."

'Vat is da matter mit you? Can't you see I'm voiking? Gay fraig dannaa Poppa.'

There was no way I was going to get her to listen to me. She was concentrating on the salad and the masses of people that would soon invade our home.

It was a standard group that once every other month stormed into our little apartment.

Isadore, the oldest, came with his second wife, Dvorah. His first wife had died on the arduous trip to New York. Pessel, the oldest sister of Pop's family, brought her husband, Jake, who never learned how to smile.

Gittel and husband, Moishe, were just nonstop laughers who shouted across the table without pause for the entire evening.

Malke, the short fat one, came alone for she was embarrassed by her foul mouthed husband.

Lisa was by far the most beautiful of all and equally sweet. She and her husband, Mendel, were as nice as could be.

Sophie, Poppa's sister and Momma's cousin and best friend, always helped the most while her husband, Izzy, spent the night frightening me by saying that if I wasn't a nice boy, they were going to send me back to Macy's where they had bought me.

The younger group was headed by Eli and his American born wife, Rachel and Zeldin, the smecker, who was the only male born in America. Zeldin deserves special attention and we will get to that later.

I never did learn the names of the Romanian non-relatives who helped fill the room.

Chapter Forty-Four

Early the next Sunday Poppa was, as usual, seated at the kitchen table and deep into his favorite newspaper, Sunday's Daily Mirror.

He did all his reading in the kitchen for it had a large window which provided great light across the kitchen table. The table was covered with his note taking.

I interrupted his concentration by asking why he seemed to scour the entire paper but never the news section. I got a one word answer.

'Ligners.'

Poppa rarely belittled anyone or anything so to hear him cry out 'liars' at such a major newspaper really threw me. My open mouth staring at him brought forth an angry second answer.

"Az mir kennisht red'n mit aleoch kite von dof nisht red'n.

Or in our tongue. "If you can't speak with truth, don't speak."

Above all Poppa deplored the word bobemeinsa. Be it in English or Yiddish it meant more than just a fairy tale. To Poppa it meant a lie, and nothing was more abhorrent to him than a falsehood. However, if the bobemeinsa led to a good punch line, all was forgiven.

That is the way he felt about his favorite newspaper.

He did not read the Daily Mirror for most of its columns were full of bobemeinsa's, but the racing pages had one punch line after the other, as it gave the results of races held the previous day. That's right, my Poppa was a horse-racing addict.

I'm sure you are wondering where he got the money to waste on that silly adventure.

Well, Poppa had developed the perfect scheme to beat the horses. He never bet a dime on any race. Instead, he kept thorough records of what he would have bet had he the money to do so.

Early on, I had become his confidant in this game he played, and he kept me advised on how much money he might have lost or won had he been a real bettor.

The smile he wore this Sunday told me that he must have done well in today's fictional wagering, and, therefore, he might be amenable to answer my query.

I was proven correct when the first words out of his mouth were *'You know somting? If I ver a richtika betta ve vud be fife hundred and tventy two dollas ahead right dis minute.'*

I didn't let his good frame of mind slip away as I let just a few moments pass by, and then asked him, for the hundredth time, my favorite question.

"Poppa, I have asked you this question before, and you never answered. But, today you must help me. I hate my first name and I want to change it."

'You don't like Dieter so change it into anudder name.'

I wasn't the dumbest kid in the world so I knew I had to question him further.

"But Poppa, why did you give me that name in the first place.

'You vant to know from your name, so I vil tell you.'

No words came out as he seemed to be doing a search for what to say. I did not understand the serious frown that crossed his face.

There was a *'vel'* and an *'efshur'* and several *'vys,' until* the following flowed forth.

'I vas eight years old ven I met a nice German boy in mine school. Everyting vee liked separately, vee liked together. The more vee ver

together the more vee became de best from friends. I tink vee just loved each other. Dat boy vas the only friend I ever had. So you are born and I'm tinking you vil be mine last chance to gif an honor to mine froint.'

I could swear I saw a bit of a tear start to drop from his left eye but it never fully appeared.

"Poppa, I am sorry but I've just been thinking of myself. That is such a nice way to remember someone so important. I will keep the name. I'll ..."

'Vait a second. You should hear dis. Venever my friend would get too excited I vud call him Deitie. He vould take a giten look at me and slowly stop being a mishugana. So vy don't you tell everyvon dat your name is Deitie. Make up some Bubbamunsa about Deitie beink a Romanian poyson who vas a groiser fighta against the Germans in Vorld Vor Vun. So ve named you faw a groiser hero of Romania.'

Poppa had solved the problem. I quickly changed my name and would forever respond only to 'Deitie'.

I assured him that I loved my last name and would never be part of changing that name. I was not aware that a formidable pair, my sister, Matty and Momma, had joined forces to tell all we must shed that strange name, Sinvalorvitz.

Matty led off the battle when she, wiping away the tears from her face said, "Sinvalorvitz might be fine in Iasi where our family had lived for hundreds of years, but it is one terrible burden to carry on our shoulders in New York City."

She then followed with a sharp jab to the chin by telling us for the nth time how a nice Jewish woman, our grandmother's mother, had lived with the very Germanic name of Veisskoff for her entire life.

"She always hated that name but they kept it as a reminder of their terrible years in Germany."

Her family moved to Romania when the Germans decided to once again stage one of their periodic pogroms against their Jews.

They kept the name Veisskoff as a tribute to those who had suffered in Germany for so many years.

Matty did not spare the whip as she beat us with, "They suffered that name, and now we must honor them by modernizing our name."

She then took a large piece of paper and with a red pencil spelled out the name Veisskoff. She then shortened that word to Veiss.

And then she announced in her most dramatic manner. "And that takes us to our American name which is....White."

We were dead in the water in this battle against the two strongest women in New York.

Poppa posed one last fraga.

'Now dat ve are da Vites vil people tink vee are Goyim, and is dat such a good ting?'

Chapter Forty-Five

Poppa had two idols whom he worshipped.

They were Sholem Asch, the great Yiddish writer, and Al Jolson, the outstanding entertainer.

Asch gave him the intellect sustenance that Poppa yearned for. Jolson endeared himself to my father with his unique ability to make you laugh and cry. Was that a strange coupling?

Oh yes, Oh yes, Oh yes. But that was my Poppa.

Asch was born just a few years prior to my father in the city of Kutno, Poland which had a sizeable and pro-active Jewish population.

As a more than brilliant teenager, Asch supported himself by being the anonymous author for all the illiterates of his community. His clients could not write in either Polish, Yiddish or Hebrew, so Asch earned a fair amount of money by being their always available scribe.

At a very early age, he had become a noted, and well-read, Hebrew writer. Fortunately, he was advised to drop Hebrew and instead write in the more popular Yiddish language. His fame grew worldwide with that switch and his career bloomed.

Poppa had five of Asch's works and coveted each one. He didn't need any more because he was constantly rereading the few he had.

To this day I recall the title of those books.

His favorite book was *Kidusha-Shem.* It was a study of the anti-Jewish uprising of the seventeenth century in Poland and the Ukraine.

I knew I should ready myself for yet another lesson whenever Poppa started a sentence with something like, *'As Sholem says in his Kidusha-Shem.'*

He would then go to his very small library and pull out a copy of that book. Poppa would spin though several pages of the book until he came upon the proper passages and then began to fiercely read aloud the words he wanted to emphasize.

Poppa didn't dwell on the wanton stupidity of Jews who hated when Asch's words cried out for every Jew to fight fiercely against the constant slaughter of their brethren.

"Foist of all they didn't know from the genius of dat mensch. Ve should have taut them dat every Jew who loifed away from da vor hundreds of der own people ver gehagered. With each Jew that flew off they lost visdom, laughter and the opportunity for a normal life any ver. It's vat ve did ven ve came here."

He often ranted on that we Jews were a rare asset to the entire world, but we were all too ready to accept bereavements but never stood up to fight for the good we brought to this world.

'Ober dey ver so rong. Der whole vorld becomes beser ven ve fight against der killers. Den da whole vorld can injoy a siesa life.'

From words like that, he taught me that standing upright is a powerful weapon. We, as Jews, must be the first to show we believe in the worth of the whole world. If we can really believe in ourselves, maybe the rest of the world would join with us in the reality of a heaven on earth.

He added that it was not that we were better than others, but it certainly was that we were no worse.

The other books were *Farm Mabul which describes* 20th century Jewish life in St. Petersburg, Warsaw and Moscow. *Ayrn Opgrunt,* set in Germany during the time of the inflation days of the 1920's, which definitely led to the rise of Adolph Hitler, and Dos *Geang Fun Tol told* us of the early Jewish settlers in Palestine.

Poppa was twenty when Asch wrote *God of Vengeance.* Fast upon the release of the book in Yiddish, it was published in German, Russian, Polish, Hebrew, Italian, Czech and Norwegian. Three years later it was adapted for a production on the New York Yiddish stage.

The play presented a look at a coarse world that featured lesbians and much sexual adventures.

Fortunately for Poppa, the theatre was located just around the corner from where we lived. In his usual manner, Poppa exchanged his altering a suit for the manager of the theatre and, in return, got a free ticket to opening night.

He could not have been more excited about going to his first theatrical production. He couldn't know that it would also be the only serious work he would see.

We were all waiting up to hear what he had to say about this surely great work from the pen of Asch. Instead he was morose in his one-sentence description of the show.

'It vas doity, doity, doity. Such a man should not have done such a roten ting.'

Poppa's review was spot on for the next day the show was shut down by the New York Police.

Each member of the cast was arrested and jailed. Despite the books worldwide acclaim, its blatant obscenity, which featured a brothel and a lesbian couple, was too much for New York's or Poppa's approval.

As was his wont, Asch never apologized for his work. The closest he came to same was one quote he issued, "People should look beyond their own little world."

Chapter Forty-Six

Think of a man who brought tears to your eyes as he sang, or had you screaming in the aisles when he donned Blackface, and you have Jolie, the second hero of my father and more importantly, Poppa's boss, Mr. Rosenthal.

Mr. R. purchased two tickets for each of Al Jolson's shows. One ticket was for himself and one for Schmuel, his key employee. He did so, for they both laughed and cried throughout each Jolson performance, and, secondly, it earned the assurance that his key employee, Sam the Tailor, would never leave Rosenthal and Sons.

Jolson and his brother, Harry, had burst forth from singing for pennies on the streets of New York. Harry handled the business end of this thing called show business, and Al developed his craft to the point where he was recognized as the all-time Master of Broadway and the entertainment world.

Al Jolson had the unique ability of walking out on any stage and within moments proving, yet again, that he was the world's greatest comedian, as well as being a man who would break your heart by singing a song that could bring tears to your eyes.

Handkerchiefs were torn out of the pockets of the most sophisticated in the audience no matter what their religion when he sang *'My Yiddisha Mamma.'*

Year after year, Al Jolson ruled the entertainment world with the words 'You ain't heard nothin yet.'

The theatre full of voices joined in wild applause as they plead for more of same.

This émigré from Srednick, Lithuania had, bit by bit, captured the entertainment world.

He was acclaimed as a born comedian, and his voice dared any other singer to match him in any form of singing. He loved everyone seated in front of him, and they more than adored him in return.

Poppa came home from an evening with Jolson ready to enthrall us with his version of the wonder of what he had just witnessed. But, often, on his late night return from such a performance, he would rapidly retire to bed, for he needed a day of rest before revealing what he had seen.

To our father, what Jolson had delivered was like a message from the heavens. Relaying the Jolson message meant having to be in in the best of form. On the next evening we all gathered in our living room awaiting Poppa's return from work.

Poppa entered our house prepared to deliver a complete report on what Jolson had done the night before.

Mama would listen from the kitchen. Matty sat at Poppa's feet, and the boys would lie on the floor all around Poppa.

Poppa would then give his version of every joke Jolson made, followed by a taste of every song Jolson had uttered. This in a cracked voice that defied any positive reaction, yet we all responded with great cheers.

Though Poppa was no Jolie, his report was a humble tribute to the talent of the great man.

We adored every second of, as he said, *'Vat Jolie did for me.'*

Despite his limited abilities, the family would scream out with pleasure, thereby showing the deep appreciation we held for our 'Jolie Sinalo…, Oh, do forgive me…Jolie White.'

Chapter Forty-Seven

I adored my Poppa probably more than he cared for his Poppa. Yet despite that love I always wondered if he ever had a serious conversation with anyone. It wasn't until I was much older that I would dare to ask my father about his perpetual silence.

Poppa sloughed it off with a few words, merely saying that he had always been a person of few words and that his nickname in Iasi had been 'The Quiet One.' And he liked being called that.

You should also know that this sweet man's work schedule was almost obscene. He left the house at seven a.m. and did not return until nine p.m, Monday to Saturday, and on alternate Sundays from ten a.m. to four p.m.

Typical of his never complaining of anything, he simply nodded his head when Momma announced her latest triumph, as she told the family that we were next moving to 239 East Fifth Street.

The new apartment was always a bit nicer than its predecessor, but hardly where she wanted to be. We would always be ready to move to a better home.

Giving birth to her sixth child, which happened to be me, from the fifth floor of a five-storied no- elevator building was more exercise than any of our family needed. Do know that every one of the babies born into our family arrived in Momma's and Poppa's bedroom.

In her continuing search for a better place for her family she ultimately found a lovely apartment which was much bigger and was in Brighton Beach, just a few blocks away from the beach -- and from our third story apartment, you could see the Atlantic Ocean.

Of course our apartment was on the top floor.

Could they afford it? No.

Poppa never raised his voice against this added burden in his already frenetic life.

Now he would normally get home sometime after ten. His sagging body and sad face instantly told you how spent he was. I cannot remember a time when he wasn't tired.

It took him at least two hours to travel to and from where he worked. Add the six hours of sleep he tried to get each night, the time to eat, escape to the peace of the bathroom, wash, undress or dress and spend a few moments with his wife, all of which left us the pleasure of his company for almost no time each day.

As soon as he entered the house, he would always go into the bathroom, which no one else dared enter between nine and ten.

Since we all arrived home for our evening meal at different times, our mother would have made individual dinners for each of us and then put together a measly platter of food ready for him when he crawled home each night.

He loved a dish called 'brains' which I could barely look at and is what she prepared for him most evenings. Whatever it was that she offered up, he never ate all on the plate.

My favorite story about him occurred one winter night. It had started snowing early one morning and by the time he got ready to leave work that night all the subways had been shut down. So what did my frail and tired father do?

He walked home.

I am talking about a five hour walk. It was just after one o'clock in the morning that the front door opened up. Every inch of him was covered with snow. He took off all his clothes, put on his pajamas and climbed into bed. The next morning he got up at seven A.M. and was back at work by nine. It took two Sundays before I could ask him what had driven him to walk home that snow-ridden night and, as per usual, his response was simple.

"Dis is my house. Dis is ver I sleep. So I vent home."

In my mind, he had just given me lesson number four hundred and twelve which is you do what you have to do and you don't make a big tsimmes about it.

Chapter Forty-Eight

Poppa always had dreams about going to school and becoming a teacher or getting a job with the government which would allow him to help straighten out the problems that faced the poor people of New York.

That is exactly what they were, dreams.

Much as he dreamed otherwise, he too knew that his every-day fight for money would be a constant deterrent to his being anything but a humble tailor. The pay he earned was far from good, but it kept the family alive.

Despite the trying times, he seemed to still love everyone he knew, with but one exception.

In private conversation with Molly, he noted that he liked how all the brides and grooms in the family were marrying away at a ferocious speed. The only groom he disliked was the man Sophie took.

"Belief me, Molly, he is a good for nothing, and Sophie is not going to have a wonderful time mit him. He talks like he knows everyting in der vorld and tinks he is God's gift to vomen. I don't tink he vil ever stop telling me how many girlfriends he left mit a tsbroachena hartz.'

Molly knew he was right and that the real reason for that marriage was Sophie's settling for the first man she could pin down. In the years following their respective marriages, my Mom had nothing but good words for her perfect husband, while Sophie never had anything to say about her man.

At about the same time, Poppa stumbled upon an event that would change my life.

He was marking up both leg lengths of a much favored customer who had one leg quite a bit longer than the other. The customer loved talking away while Poppa was hard at work 'chalking up' his two uneven pant legs.

He once told Poppa that each summer he and several of his friends put together a rather large sum of money that enabled them to send some twenty-five boys and girls to a camp on Sugar Loaf Mountain in Maine.

"I tell you, Sam, we take these kids who haven't ever been out of the city and put them in a learning situation that is unbelievable. In one-half day they might be climbing up four thousand feet where they would spend hours discussing Chaucer, while at the same time they would be cooking their own meals for lunch and dinner."

The customer went on about how the students came back far brighter and stronger from this summer that stressed both the cerebral and the physical.

"The kids we select have just finished their High School Sophomore year and had to have proven intellectual and personal traits that showed they had leadership potential."

"Dat's a wonderful ting you are doing. How do you get the boys you have to choose from?"

"That is a good question, Sam, for it is a difficult chore. Every school principal in the city is solicited and allowed to offer several names from his school, who they believe are capable of surviving the strenuous program we offer. Each of our board members can offer up a name or two. I haven't decided who I will name this year."

Pop heard those words and jumped right in.

"May I tell you about mine son who is as poifect as any stitch I have ever sewn. He is the smartest one in his class and vas just chosen to be the class president next year. I don't like to be a boaster but I tell you none of dem have a kop like mine boy."

To this day, I do not know whether it was Pop's client's desire to keep my father as his tailor or that I really did well on the test and the interview, but I was accepted for the program.

I was both frightened and delighted with what I was about to face, which is an understatement of vast proportions.

It would be the first time that I would be away from my Brooklyn. To do so without any of my family with me was more than frightening.

But what a glorious two months they were. I grew in every manner, as we discussed subjects I had never even thought of all the while learning how to cook meals that were at least edible. I came away in love with everyone at the camp and, yes, there was one special young girl who occupied my every thought.

I learned that I had one serious problem. Being a student at Brooklyn Technical High School, which had only male students, I could only blush or stammer when faced with my new companions, called 'girls.'

I returned smarter and stronger yet still a virgin.

Chapter Forty-Nine

Let me introduce yet another family that was most important in our lives.

Now, typical of the very complex inter-marriages that were so common in those days, I must detail a few of those marriages and some of the children that came forth from those bondages.

Asser S. married Yettie K. this marriage produced a ton of children including Schmuel and and Sophie.

Duvid married Sarah K. They produced Molly and two boys.

Asser had a youngest sister named Ethel.

Molly, Sophie, and their friend Ida were a fearsome team who used Ethel to solve any of the many battles they fought. Ethel loved being the big sister to those silly kids.

Jake Rubitz met Ethel at a Rosh Hashana service. This led to two important events. He got a job at Asser's store, and she had little time for the girls any longer.

Jake eventfully proved to be a most successful salesman who drove every one of his fellow workers somewhat mad. He would constantly be telling everyone from Asser to Schmuel how things should be done to better the store.

Not many months later, Jake became obsessed with creating a business akin to what Asser had created in Iasi.

The courtship between Ethel and Jake did not last long. They soon were married despite the pleadings of Asser to his young sister that Jake was a 'definite mishigina'.

Their wedding gift from Asser was sufficient Leis for their honeymoon which took them out of Romania and permanently to America.

He was nineteen and she was sixteen. They left Iasi long before many of its residents had even thought of moving away from their homeland.

By the age of twenty three, he had found a job at a small men's store. His best friend at the store was an equally aggressive young man, also from Romania. It was not too much later that they opened their own clothing store, "Jake and Barney's."

They remained friends for the rest of their lives but found their constant arguments too difficult to sustain in a business. Barney moved West and Jake moved south.

Both men were oddly idiosyncratic….wait a second…..by the time I met them they were just two wacky old men, so cancel that word.

One day Jake took me to Barney's store. The men hugged each other and were seemingly enjoying this surprise visit.

Barney was more than gracious to Jake, and Jake was equally nice to his old friend and ex-partner.

They were two wacky men past their prime, yet each shared the same dream. They still longed to be the owners of the most successful small clothing store in the world.

The smiles lasted for about fifteen minutes when Jake, looking up and down the rather empty aisles, said the following.

"Vat's mit der lousy business, Barnala?"

That was it. Barney countered with the claim that they did more business in one hour than Jake did in a week.

To which Jake said, "Sure. Dats because you give away your phastinkina clothes."

Young as I was, I knew enough to thank Barney and drag Jake out of the store.

Neither one fulfilled their dream. Each store grew modestly, until their first sons took over the entire business. Thereafter, the growth was much more noticeable.

Which brings us to Buddy Ruditz, the oldest son of Jake and Ethel, who was the catalyst for the small success that came along.

I have never seen or heard anyone as handsome, nor as glib, as Buddy was. If he deigned to work with a special customer, there was little doubt that the customer would buy far more than he started out to.

If the customer was a bit doubtful, Buddy would don the jacket, no matter the size, while telling the customer, "Look at this suit. It is you, and you are gorgeous."

Buddy worked very hard, but his vulnerability emerged when a customer entered the store with a pretty woman at his side.

Buddy loved women and had to conquer each one he met. So he sold the woman on how great he was, rather than how great her husband looked in the new suit Buddy was trying to sell him.

By the time I had arrived on the scene, Buddy, the older son, had taken over total command of the store.

Deep down, Buddy was an actor yearning for his moment on the stage. To see him make a sale was like watching someone vying for an Academy Award.

Was he good at the job? NO! He was merely sensational.

Buddy deserved all the kudos he received.

As part of his artistic side, Buddy also liked to dress the stores windows, and he was quite good at doing so. Since the store was graced with huge windows on two sides, it was an important sales tool that the windows looked great.

But should Jake see Buddy dressing a window, he would scream out, no matter how crowded it was in the store, "Vy vaste dinor tseit in da vindo. Call a person who does dat. Pay him ten dollars and you try to tink and come up mit an idea that might sell some clothes."

Buddy, of course, ignored him.

Let me add a bit of sanity to this ensemble. That would be Joey, Jake and Ethel's other child.

He always set an absolutely pleasant tone. In all his business doings he was always the most affable and kind to everyone. It was a pleasure to work with him or to be the customer who was trying to buy a new suit at a fair price.

Joey did not look like his older brother. Did not have his wit and, I assure you, had but one woman in his life. He married her and never thought about another woman.

One just had to love that man. He never argued with anyone. He never over-sold a customer.

Yes, he was ineffectual as compared to Buddy but, contrary to all the other wackos who populated the store, he was a pleasure throughout every day.

I had a variety of chores in this madhouse. They ranged from straightening out the hanging suits, sweeping the two level store, packing all the sold goods, rushing out to perform some strange errand or redoing something I had just done to perfection, constantly running out to buy coffee for Jake and his two sons and, most importantly, to respond as quickly as I could to a scream from anyone.

"Dietie, I need you. Now!"

It was very difficult for me to determine who was craziest of the screamers, for their quest was never anything of dire need.

Chapter Fifty

Their store on Broadway's lower Manhattan did a fair business but really blossomed when it moved, at Buddy's advice, twenty-six streets up Broadway.

Jake had long since been barred from dealing with a customer. Instead, he could sit or stand near the front of the store, but he was never allowed to say a word that might be overheard.

Strangely enough he always adhered to that dictum which had been laid down by Buddy.

Jake's favorite expression was one we heard ten or twelve times a day.

"Vatch out for dat vun, He's a guaranteed gonif, a shop lifter."

He was always on the alert for those thieves who, in his mind, were constantly invading his store.

If we were all busy he would trail an unattended shopper and wait to catch him in the act of stealing a tie or a belt or, worst of all, an overcoat. Was he certifiable? Of course.

My opinion on the matter was that he should be just left alone. He rarely caused any trouble and he took care of a real problem.

Ethel!

Her one purpose in life was to come to the store each day prepared to serve up lunch for all her men. As long as Jake was ever present, Ethel would be in the store quietly ready to take care of her brood.

Nobody said a word to Ethel, as she sat in the little office near the front entrance. She, on the other hand, continually asked her men if they were hungry yet.

Another notable was our tailor, Mischa, who also had a screw loose.

I would not put him close to the other crazies in that store, but I must present the argument that might indicate some things askew in his mental processing.

Many times he would rush out of his little room in the back of the store and race to the pay phone where he would, as fast as possible, insert a coin and then whistle away while waiting for someone to answer his call.

The next words uttered by Mischa were loud enough to be heard throughout the store and down the street. "Dis is Mischa. Can you hear me?"

Obviously Mischa had no faith in AT&T.

"Yes, and I vant right avay a cup of empty coffee. I said empty coffee. Dats right, empty coffee. No, I vant it now. Tank you."

I never understood why he had to shout his message, since it went out at least four times a day to the same ears.

Ten minutes later a short man would run into the store carrying a large cup of coffee. He would race to Mischa's room, and a few minutes later he would race out of the store. He never spoke a word as he broke speeding records in his dashing in and out.

What is a cup of empty coffee?

It is a full cup of black coffee with no milk, sugar or anything that might alter the taste.

I imagine whoever answered that call knew what the hell Mischa was saying, but it took me many moons before a) I understood what he asked for and b) the why of it all.

And then there was Izzy.

He was Jake's only friend. When Jake fled to America, Izzy also left Iasi. Izzy was tiny and had the strangest speech pattern I ever heard. He was one of the oddest looking men I had ever seen with a huge nose, a tiny mouth and eyes that were constantly racing from side to side.

His hair was always wild and his clothes never matched.

We would never know when Izzy would show up at the store. Sometimes he would be waiting in front of the store before it opened, and, at other times, he would arrive just before we closed.

I knew he held a job somewhere, but what he did, no one ever said. I gathered that one day he quit his job and became a permanent fixture at the store.

Oddly enough, nobody ever gave him a hard time.

If there were a line of customers waiting to be served, Izzy was allowed to escort the one waiting the longest to the suit area.

Buddy had taught him one sentence he could say to a customer, "These are your sizes, and a salesman will be right with you."

He then would hasten back to his favorite spot, the chair next to Jake. He would spend his time there nodding his head at everything Jake said.

Ethel never made him a sandwich.

So I never did learn anything of substance about the clothing business, other than how to keep a hangar straight so that the item it carried wouldn't slip off and fall to the floor.

No matter how many times Buddy and I would walk up and down the suit aisles and mark up the sales tags, I never came up with any logic that led to the final sales price.

Each tag would have an official looking marking that said its original price would range from $150 to $250. The sales price would depend on how Buddy felt that morning.

His favorite marking was that all suits that day only were on sale at half the price listed. What a steal.

What astonished me was how very few customers questioned the fraudulent listed price. The sales people knew only one thing mattered.

'Make the sale at our price.'

Chapter Fifty-One

Nobody said a word to Ethel, as she sat in the little office near the front entrance. She, on the other hand, continually asked her men if they were hungry yet. That continued until she got bored when she would shout out, "Da Sandviches are ready come and eat.

Sometimes that feast would just linger away totally untouched.

Buddy had gotten his parents into a really neat apartment house in Brighton Beach. He did so in the hope that this glamorous apartment would keep them at home a greater part of the day.

He failed. Jake made a deal with a local taxi service that picked him and Ethel up at nine A.M. and delivered them to the store a bit after ten.

Jake and Ethel lived in this wonderful new and huge six-story building that looked directly across the street from an old three- story building, where we occupied the top floor.

I never knew if we had brought Jake and Ethel to where we lived, or did they bring us to where they lived? It mattered little, but I bet it was Ethel who dragged little Molly across town.

It was very easy to see if Ethel was home, for when she was, she would be sitting in her bedroom window with her arms folded and her head sticking straight out, as she kept tabs on Molly's whereabouts.

Somehow, Ethel survived with a definitively mad husband. I always thought she was a bit daffy as well, but she was always so sweet that I never voiced that.

Momma's opinion was often bluntly laid out.

"Dat voman is taka a mischigina. Did ve get a phone just so dat she could keep calling me to drive me mischiga too?"

Poppa's take on that family was even better.

"Dey are a tousent times richer den ve are, and ve are a million times happier than they could ever be."

This was only said when Momma had to hang up the phone while Ethel just kept on talking.

She never voiced a word about the business. Her mission in life seemed to be that she never allowed her husband or children to starve to death.

She cared for nothing but her husband and her children.

In the years I worked there, I was never offered an apple or a cookie or anything edible. In addition, I don't believe she ever spoke to me, other than to tell me to get the seltzer water for her Jake.

I was twenty six year old when I made a gross error. I introduced the woman of my dreams, Marnie, to this mad family.

Talk about two cultures both trying to get along with one another, but failing to do so.

Ethel decided to only speak in Yiddish to this nice Christian girl. Marnie would politely nod her head in agreement to whatever it was that had just been said to her.

Ethel, for all her craziness, was a seriously great cook. Welcoming Marnie, she invited her and the rest of us to a meal that featured noodle kugel and kasha varnishkas. They were both beyond delicious.

Marnie, as always gracious, asked Ethel how to cook these amazing dishes.

Ethel's response was, "Oy vey is mir. It's so easy." She then turned away from Marnie.

There were many opportunities for Marnie to ask that question again and she always received the same answer, "Oy vey is mir. It's so easy."

This equaled Momma's answer to Marnie's question about putting radishes in the Potla Gel.

"If you got it put it in."

Marnie finally gave up on both women but not before telling me that Jewish women were sure jealous about their recipes.

Chapter Fifty-Two

Let me take you back to Buddy.

At that time, he was the only one I knew who owned a car. So when I was due to work at the store, he would pick me up at our house and we would get to the store in about a half hour. It meant getting to and from the store each Saturday and Sunday a breeze for me.

One Saturday, on the way home, he brought up a discussion he never had opened before. He looked me straight in the eye and asked if I had noticed a very pretty young woman who had been in the store that afternoon.

Noticed! What a joke.

Did I notice her?

No, I spent the time scratching my nose as I slowly crept nearer and nearer to that ugly old man. Are you crazy? That woman had mesmerized me. I had never seen anything as beautiful as that woman whom I hardly noticed.

I looked Buddy straight in the eye and exclaimed, "Noticed her. I nearly died staring at every part of her."

Buddy had been working very slowly with an elderly man and a gorgeous young woman. He had just handed me four of our most costly suits while telling me to make sure I gave it the A-One packing treatment.

"Be careful to pack them slowly. They need the best attention you can give them."

As I neared the checkout counter the woman had strolled past me on her way out the front door. Accidently, I think, she brushed against my right arm.

My eyes did a triple take, my nose whiffed an aroma that was beyond belief, and I almost dropped each of those suits.

The three of them had been together for some time and no one in the store did anything but stare at them as the man had tried on suit after suit.

Buddy laughed and then said the most important words I had ever heard in my entire life.

"How would you like me to get her to take care of you?"

Right there. At that very moment, I nearly had a heart attack. Being uncertain I asked him what he meant by the words 'take care of me?'

He didn't reply. He just winked at me as he said, "The deed will be done next Saturday. You'll be spending some time with her down in the storage room."

I died many times the next week. I thought about her. I dreamt about her. I failed two tests because of her and Momma, on Tuesday night, asked if I felt all right because I didn't look to good. I assured her that all was well with me.

I hardly slept that Friday night. I swallowed my Saturday morning breakfast and within minutes of doing so I was outside waiting to be picked up by Buddy.

It took me a long while to realize that his normal pick up time was still forty five minutes away.

Finally he did arrive. He was as full of it as ever. We spent most of the time talking about Mel Ott and Bill Terry of the New York Giants baseball team. He was a big fan of the Brooklyn Dodgers while I was a Giants fan.

He did not mention one word about what was to be my fate that day.

The discussion about the Giants being a much better team than the woeful Dodgers continued as I tried to think of something to say that lead us into a more interesting subject. Sex.

But I could not come with a single thought and dear Uncle Buddy was apparently content with talk about baseball.

Not a word was spoken about a certain woman.

She was not brought up again for the remainder of the day nor was she brought up on the trip home.

I was a bit disappointed but consoled myself as I remembered that she had been at the store on the previous Sunday. Tomorrow would be my day of total delight.

That day arrived and that day ended without a word from Buddy about you know who.

As a matter of fact he never raised the subject again, and I hated him for many years. At the very least he could have lied and told me she had died or she and her old husband had flown to some foreign capital.

But no. In fact he left me thinking that said conversation had never happened. I was so angry that I would never give him the satisfaction of even asking him about her.

Forever later, when I had long since forgiven Buddy for the cruelty he had imposed on a hungry and innocent young fourteen year old, he closed the store.

Instead he decided that he had worked long enough and hard enough for others so, at the age of sixty-eight, he decided he was an actor.

Damned if he didn't get to play a small role in a Broadway play that bombed. Had several tiny parts in any number of television series. And, his biggest success was as spokesman for a large number of TV commercials. I loved everything he did, and I even forgave him for the pain he put me through when I was fourteen years old.

Chapter Fifty-Three

As I spent most of my day studying what my father did I became curious about a weird activity he pursued daily.

This odd happening began with Momma making a small package each morning before Poppa left for work. He would grab same package as he rushed through the kitchen and headed out the front door.

Since Momma never would tell me what was in the packet he carried off, I couldn't resist asking him about said contents.

"Poppa, what do you take from the kitchen table every morning?"

"Dat's my Chinese lunch. Momma makes me a wonderful sandwich."

"Momma can cook Chinese food?"

"Ven did I say she could do dat?"

"You just said it was your Chinese lunch."

"I didn't say I ate Chinese food. I just eat the sandwich in a Chinese movie theatre."

"You what?"

He then went on in great detail explaining that promptly at twelve o'clock each day he would walk four blocks from where he worked to the edge of Chinatown. At the first corner he walked into a small Chinese movie theatre.

"As I enter the theatre I vave to the Chinese girl who vas da cashier and she vaves beck to me. The seat I sit in is the first seat in the beck row. Already in the arm of the seat is a paper cup filled with vasser."

"Wait, wait, wait. Is there a movie running at that time?"

"Certainly, why would all the Chinese people be seated there if nothing was running?"

"Poppa, do you know the Chinese language?"

"No. I just go there to eat my sandwich."

"But why do you go to a Chinese Theatre to eat a sandwich?"

"Because it is quiet and cool, and I don't have to talk to anyone there and the owner of the theatre, who is Chinese and a vunderful mensch, is one of my best customers. He asked me to come to his theatre, and he would tell all of his workers to treat me nicely and not charge me anything."

About an hour after entering the theatre, Poppa, as always an absolute gentleman, would greet the ever curious Chinese folk surrounding him. He would extend a gracious smile and, in the best of Yiddish, say, *'A giten tog. Zie gezinte.'*

Since Poppa never told me the moral of each of his bizarre doings, the entire story took me a longtime to decipher.

I came up with many flawed reasons for my father eating lunch in a Chinese movie house. Here is my offering as to what I believe is the closest to the truth.

His client would feel good about an American patronizing his theatre. The customers in the theatre would be happy in thinking that even non-Chinamen could enjoy their movies.

On finishing his lunch, he would walk to the owner's office and thank the owner for the delightful hour he spent in the theatre.

Everyone would be happy. Above all, it would be my father that was happiest of them all.

Can you come up with a better rationale?

Chapter Fifty-Four

Not a one in our family sweated being poor. Every family living in our neighborhood suffered from the same lack of money that we did.

Playing stick ball in the streets was rarely interrupted by a car driving down our streets. We did not know of anyone who owned a car.

My best friend was Marty Goldstein. He was as crazy as could be and always the winner in every game we played.

Whether it was 'Three feet off to Germany,' or 'Horse,' or 'Street Punch Ball,' or just the simplest game of 'Tag,' Marty won the game, and if you were lucky enough to be on his side, you were a winner too.

There was no question about who the leader of our gang was. Lucky for the rest of us menials, Marty was a gentle leader.

Those were wonderful days.

One day the guys, of course led by Marty, were playing war games in the empty lot at the end of our street. The next day he was gone.

We later heard that his father had lost his job, and they were living in a tenement in the poorest section of Brooklyn.

You don't know what the word tenement means? It was akin to slum housing for the very poor.

Yes, sometimes people like Marty, would be here one day then suddenly disappear. It wasn't until I was a freshman at Brooklyn College, some ten years later, that I saw him again.

He was a wearing a U.S. Navy uniform, and when I rushed up to him with great joy ready to give him a big bear hug, he backed away from me. He didn't say 'Hi,' or anything else.

Yes, The Great Depression had killed my friend Marty. He should have ended up as a hero. Instead he was ashamed of himself and what the world had led him to be.

Chapter Fifty-Five

One day I had a big fight with my second best friend in Brighton Beach. I remember his name was Marvin, but I don't have a clue as to what we were arguing about. The only thing I remember is that he was one year younger than me.

I assume he said something that I didn't like, so I felt it was necessary to straighten out this young kid and, therefore, I punched him in the nose.

Marvin cried and ran away from me. I thought I would be proud of what I did but I really felt sad about it.

I asked Poppa to explain all of that to me.

'Certainly, but foist I vil tell you of a grosertsur tsoura vich appened on Frituk.'

I could sense he was searching for words, for it took him quite some time before he started speaking again.

'I come home from voik and I go into my betroom ver Momma is sitting. I start to take off mine jacket ven I look at the bet. Ver dar vonce was mine bet which Momma and I had slept in all our life, and I don't see it. Instead I see two small beds with a table between them. I look and look and den I finally fraig dina Momma, Vat is dis? You know some times your Momma ken be a tough lady and vat she said proves that.'

He then turns to me and with the saddest face I have ever seen tells me how Momma explained what happened that morning.

"Momma vent to the department store, John Vanamaker. She tells the man dere dat if he can bring two of the beds she likes to her house today and takes the old bed away, he has a deal. And then Momma says to me. 'And dats it and dat's all.'"

I asked him if he didn't try to do something or say something to get rid of those beds.

"Vat else could I do. I look vonce den noch amule at the new bets and den I know der is noughtink I can do so I turn to your mother and I shout out very strong, GOD DAMN VANAMAKER."

And from that episode in his life came lesson number four hundred and thirteen.

One may shout out but what means something to the shouter, is just noise to the person who has been shouted at. And that is what happened with Marvin.

Marvin had run from me because he didn't like all the noise I was making.

Some twenty five years went by since I punched Marvin. I am walking down Fifth Avenue when a man taps me on the shoulder and says, "Excuse me, but is your name Dietie?"

That's right, it was Marvin -- but not the skinny little kid I knew in Brighton Beach. This guy must have been about six foot two in height and weighed in at least two hundred and ten pounds.

Fortunately he didn't remember the noise I made that day. What we talked about for over a half hour was how lucky we were to have been brought up in Brighton Beach and what great friends we had been in those days.

Chapter Fifty-Six

May I introduce you to Mendel Schwartz. He was born in Iasi but his family moved from Romania before he turned two.

Mendel was some five years older than Poppa, who he met when they both attended a meeting of the Romanian Association.

The lure for both men was that the Association had burial grounds for its members and their families.

Of course he had never learned the Romanian language, and though he was Jewish, he hadn't been exposed to Yiddish at all.

He had two older sisters, but somehow there had been a serous falling out between Mendel and his entire family. We did get to meet them and they seemed quite nice. We never learned about their split.

All we knew was that he had left his family in his early twenties and had spent the years since carousing as best as he could. He was a bachelor and not the nicest of men but he came up with an interesting offer.

"Listen, Sam, I have a problem right now. I lost a little apartment I lived in and need a place to stay. If you have a spare room to let, I would love to pay you whatever you want for it."

This was hardly a fresh idea, for most families in my neighborhood had at least one 'Boarder,' who was usually a man with no family, who needed a place to live.

I overheard many a fierce discussion between Poppa and Momma when they tried to decide what to do about Mendel's offer.

Each agreed that we could use the extra money but were concerned about the impact he would have on our very tight-knit family.

"Ve should for take him in. It vil make things beser fur der kinda.

At one point I heard Momma cry out that we did not celebrate the holiday, Chanukah, because that meant giving Chanukah Gelt which we couldn't afford.

The thought of a stranger in their house irked them, but the extra money would put them in an apartment they loved.

Money won out.

Chapter Fifty-Seven

Schwartz was a waiter at many of the better night clubs that opened and closed with great rapidity in the dazzling nightlife of the city.

He never came home before one or two in the morning but, to his credit, no one ever heard him come in at that hour.

His ritual was to sleep until nine or ten, and he would leave the house no later than one P.M.

However, Schwartz annoyed us with his non-stop ability to forever keep talking, mostly about himself. No one ever mentioned it, but I think we all resented his being a member of our dining room on festive occasions.

Because of his crazy hours, Momma, my brother, Willie, and that brat of the clan, me, were the only ones who were exposed to his verbiage.

For reasons that I never fathomed, I was the only one that tolerated him. My brothers really hated him. Matty could have easily shot him. Momma took him in stride.

But it was Poppa who, after a very short spell, outwardly loathed him. Psychologically, easy to understand.

The entire family celebrated when November would arrive, and he left for a job in Florida. April always came too soon for it brought Mendel back to us, and we lost our spare bed room.

This in turn meant Matty had to once again sleep in the living room. To her deserved credit, she never made an issue of that. We really appreciated that.

One afternoon, I wandered into his room, and, for no reason whatsoever, I opened his bureau drawers. All I found was the usual assortment of underwear, socks etc.

But when I reached the bottom drawer I found a collection of what used to be called dirty books. And on top of them a package whose name I can't recall but which was highlighted by the words 'Get them to eat this, and they'll do anything you want them to.'

Of course that drove me to Buddy that night for an explanation of my discovery.

First, he severally lambasted me for what I had done.

"How dare you sneak into Mendel's room? You are a rotten little snoop, and if I hear of you doing something like that ever again, I will whip you as hard as I can."

How I got the courage to ask another question after that shows how great my curiosity was.

"I apologize, Buddy. I promise I will never do that again.'

But being a persistent bugger, I forced Buddy to give me an explanation of that package.

Buddy tried to be stern about not answering my question, but after my fourth 'Aw c'mon,' he yielded and told me that's what dirty old men would use to get dirty things done.

That of course revealed nothing to me except that Mendel was not a nice guy.

Every now and then Mendel would take me to the hot baths in Coney Island. Most of the men there were firemen and not one of them was Jewish.

His tendency to lie was made clear to me when he would introduce me as his son and then tell me to jump into the pool and swim as fast as I could. I would do so not knowing what the devil I was proving until I finished the lap and got out to hear him say, "That's my kid. He is going to be a champion swimmer."

I never understood why he would pose that blatant lie, but I just let it pass.

Anyway, my real father never lied and was much nicer than our Boarder.

Mendel Schwartz lived with us for over twenty years.

I once asked my mother what I should call him when someone asked about him. Her response was as quick as can be.

"All dey have to know is dat he lives mit us. You don't know notink about him."

I wondered why he didn't live with his sisters but never got an answer about that.

Many years later Mendel Schwartz contracted Prostate Cancer. As soon as I could, I raced to the dreadful hospital he was confined to. I was the only one to visit him.

He lay perfectly still in a room full of others in exactly the same state. The hospital was, at best, woefully sordid. I am certain he did not know I had come to see him. I stayed but a few minutes with the poor man.

He would die the very next day with no one but me to honor him with a visit.

Upon hearing the news, my father's comment was simply, "I never thought I would live longer than dat man."

Which showed me how much it had bothered my father to gather in Mendel's weekly cash payments.

Neither Momma nor Poppa ever talked about Mendel's death.

The more I think about it the more I realize that the only involvement that Sam had with our family is that for seven months of the year he slept in the same apartment that we did.

Chapter Fifty-Eight

Throughout the following years Matty continued with her unbroken streak of making terrible decisions. By far the greatest mistake came with her announcement that she had decided to marry Burt, a man she had recently introduced us to.

Let me start out with a positive word or two about that man. First off he was quite handsome, and, secondly, he had a very pleasant singing voice, which he constantly regaled us with.

But for all of us, the balance between the good and the bad of that man was definitively in the negative.

Burt worked for the I.R.S.

If you listened to his words one would think he met each morning with the President Truman who daily asked for advice on how to run our country.

We all wondered if he was as big a braggart on the job as he was in our house. I might add, with just cause, that he treated all of us like underlings and he was always the king of the dance.

Most of our family's biggest gripe with the man was his never ending complaints about Momma's always serving Salad de Venita which he just could not stand.

I detested him with a much warranted passion.

One day Matty asked me why Burt thought I was deaf. I told her that I could not understand that at all. Truth of the matter was that I was sick of Burt using me like a stupid little errand boy.

I stopped that by being deaf whenever he had something to say.

My brothers made certain they were not in the house on any occasion that he and my sister were there.

Poppa found a new use for the Daily Mirror when Burt arrived. He buried himself in his bedroom with the hot news the paper was reporting on that day.

He also shared with the other men in the family in not having the strength of character to listen as Matty and Burt declaimed away about how great a catch Burt was.

It was even worse when words poured out in infinite details on the subject of their forthcoming marriage.

Mom, of course, broke the silence while giving Matty a big kiss. I was certain there was a tear or two flowing down Mom's cheek. I was equally confident they were not tears of joy.

Not a one of us could think of anything nice to say about an event joining those two.

Willie stuffed a napkin in his mouth to keep laughter from pouring out while whispering his blessings.

"Congrats to the both of you. To Matty, who now has a reason to cry all the time, as she tells the world what a great husband Burt will be, and to Burt, who, undoubtedly, will repeat the same words."

Poppa quietly muttered his way through a hug and an *'isn't dis a nice appenik'.'*

Buddy, who was normally kinder than kind to everyone, couldn't find anything to say.

'Is that going to be soon?' came out of my mouth. Shall we say it was at best nonsensical.

The wedding was held in a swank Fifth Avenue hotel. Some boring official from Burt's office read the service and fled away as soon as he proclaimed, 'I now pronounce you man and wife.'

The food was less than edible.

There was no Music, and Burt and his guests were the only ones who imbibed in what liquor was offered to all.

Willy broke us up by lifting his cocktail glass, which was filled with water, and toasting the newlyweds.

"Here's to two who deserve each other more than any that have ever been so graciously mated."

Chapter Fifty-Nine

Some Dads give their sons tons of money that enable them to be mighty successes in their life. Others put their handsome progeny into businesses that rank high in the economic future of the world.

Some introduce them to daughters of the most famed bankers or corporate leaders in the world. Others get close to political leaders who can place their beloved lineage in important positions that can lead to much wealth.

Well, my father did the same for me. Granted it was not on the same scale. He did it with men who liked good fitting clothes.

I had just gotten my Masters in Arts and Design at Hunter College in New York City. It was attained by taking each course at night school so that I could work each day at menial work that kept me almost financially viable.

In later years, I realized that said degree could not have been a bigger waste of time, as all it gave me was a piece of paper. It changed nothing in my feeble attempts to start some sort of career.

Poppa changed all of that. He embarked on his own campaign to obtain a suitable job for me. There was as little hope for his efforts to succeed as there were for mine.

However, he never stopped trying, and one day he pitched my talents to yet another of his most friendly customers.

Mr. Edward Hyman, a Senior-Vice President of the theatre division of Paramount Pictures, received a most ardent pitch from Poppa.

Amazingly, Mr. Hyman told my father that he would be happy to talk with me. Even more awesome was that shortly following that meeting, he offered me a job as a trainee. Hallelujah!

After six weeks of training at the New York and Brooklyn Paramount Theatres, I was ready for my next assignment which would send me off for further training in Salt Lake City.

Chapter Sixty

My extreme distaste for Burt began as I was about to start the greatest adventure of my young life.

I was five minutes away from boarding a plane, heading towards Salt Lake City and the second phase of learning all about the motion picture business.

My entire family was at LaGuardia Airport to see me off. To say the least, it was a very emotional moment. I was torn by the excitement of moving upward in my career but sad as all hell with the thought of leaving everybody I loved. Those were real tears in my eyes

After a thousand hugs and kisses, I turned towards the plane. From behind me, I could hear Burt laughing away.

I continued walking towards the plane and away from all my loved ones. As I neared the ramp I heard Burt shout out as loud as he could that I was a little cry baby gushing tears that showed how frightened I was about getting on the plane.

I have never been so furious in all my life. Yes, I had more than one tear gushing down my cheeks but they had nothing to do with fear but about how much I would miss those wonderful people behind me.

I stopped midway to the plane, turned back to Burt and spoke these exact words.

"No, you stupid Bastard, I'm crying because I know how much I love each of my family, and how much I will miss them. Poppa, thank you for always thinking of me. Momma, I love you, and I'll miss you every day I am gone. Buddy, Willy and Matty. You are the best. But Burt, you are a blithering idiot, I am sorry you didn't have a father and mother like I do."

Looking at my father, I instantly knew that was not the way he would have handled the situation. But, honestly, I was pleased with the expression I had left on Burt's face.

Chapter Sixty-One

Three years later two epic events happened that involved Matty and, unfortunately, me.

Of greatest significance was the fact that she decided she could not stand Burt for even one day longer.

She managed to muster the courage, with much prodding from Momma, to throw Burt out of their apartment and made plans to fly to Mexico for a quickie divorce.

I argued like all hell when Mom told me I must be the one to accompany Matty through that process for she could not do so alone.

Her reply was simple.

"Velvel and Abie are vorking so dey cannot leave their jobs. You are a big shot and you can take a couple days off. Dat means you are de lucky von. So, just be a nice boy and take care of your sister who needs you and loves you."

Don't buy into that big shot as meaning anything but that I was constantly on the road touring theatre after theatre, and I reported to no one about where or when I was going. As a matter of fact secrecy was considered to be a pertinent part of my work.

I assure you, I was not a pleasant companion, but I let Matty cry away most of each day as I procured all the necessary paper work.

Oh yes, then as now, I could not speak one word of Spanish. I assure you ordering dinner or speaking to a clerk in the court house was not an easy task.

Somehow, I survived and, I assure you, Matty returned unchanged and furious with what the world had handed her.

Not once did I get a word of thanks from Matty but Momma's thank you was full hearted as she welcomed me with,*"Look who's here, mine favrite voild travel poison?"*

Some years later we read a very interesting item in the New York Times. Burt was sent to prison for having approved many income tax reports that were obviously fraudulent. It seemed he was very well compensated for this courtesy to his clients.

To the very end, Burt kept screaming that there was no proof backing up the government's claim that he was a thief.

Somehow they mustered up enough facts to send Burt away for ten to twenty years.

As usual Poppa summed it up in two sentences.

"I vunder how de other prisoners like having Burt sing to dem?

I felt that was a fair question but not as strong a question as the second one.

"Do you tink we should send him veekly portions of Potla Jel dat he can share mit his cellmates?"

He paused for a beat or two and then asked me to complete the following.

'Vons a tsiken, alvays a tsiken.' Vons a Burt alvays a?

And I shouted as loudly as I could Burt.

"Always a Burt."

Chapter Sixty-Two

It was not too long afterward that Matty met Eddie, the antithesis of Burt. Their relationship grew close in but a few dates. We all predicted that their marriage would be quickly forthcoming. Said event occurred within six months.

I am certain that he was a good guy, and we all kind of liked him but, without a doubt, he was the dullest man I had ever met. Eddie, made my father look like a loud mouth.

He was soft spoken to a fault. A conversation with him sometimes lasted one to two minutes. But he couldn't sing a note and was rather plain looking. He had fashioned a career selling paper. Huh?

I never did discover how one sold paper. It was too complex for me.

Eddie was totally different from Burt; therefore, marrying him promised the possibility of yielding a successful marriage.

The fact that he was totally ruled by his mother, and was the dullest man in the world, was not part of Matty's cognition so, I guess, Matty suspended her doubts about Eddie and wedding plans were made.

Willie and I made a wager as to how long the coupling would last. I, the optimist, gave them at least five years, and Willie pocketed the cash with his giving them two years.

I am sure Matty would have stayed with Eddie forever. But he was the definitive mother's boy and clung to every word spoken by his mother.

That woman totally missed the boat about Matty who was light years ahead of her Eddie in every possible way.

She openly detested Matty from the day Eddie introduced the two of them. Now say what you may about my sister, she was still one smart cookie. I assure you, Matty immediately figured out the kind of broad she was facing and went out of her way to get Eddie's Mom to like her.

Talk about an impossible task. Unfortunately, she decided she could win the lady over.

Sorry, Matty, you never had a chance.

The battle ended when Matty decided that she just wouldn't let Eddie's mother start to run Matty's life as well as Eddie's.

This marriage lasted all of nineteen months and, of course, there were no progeny.

Their divorce was handled very efficiently by the third husband of Eddie's mother. We all admired what a fine attorney he was.

Eddie got off scot-free. But it was far from a total loss. Matty got to keep the new apartment they had just furnished.

Chapter Sixty-Three

Poppa and I were deep into a conversation about his methods of assessing who would win a big horse race that was to come up the following Saturday. He casually noted that the one thing that prevented his picking the winner was that you could never trust a jockey.

And then he added. "You know my little breider, Zeldin, was so tiny, he could have bin a jockey."

Mention of his little brother Zeldin allowed me to change the entire course of our conversation.

I jumped in with, "Poppa, you seldom talk about Zeldin but when you do it's always as if there was something wrong with him. I think I've seen him twice and both times he never said a word to anyone. What's his story?"

Poppa took some time before deciding to tell me about his brother. I confess I was not happy to hear it. That life had not one ounce of joy in it.

Zeldin was a lost cause from the day of his birth. He was nearly lost in the birthing process. Poppa told me that Zeldin didn't speak a word until he was three years old.

At the normal age, he was sent to Public School, but within six months, Grandma was told to keep him at home. She was told he wasn't ready for any schooling.

He was quite short and very thin so most people thought he was younger than his real age.

For many years he would just hang out on the street. Nobody talked to him or had anything to do with him.

It wasn't until he was fourteen when a local gang of bad kids, just a few years older than him, discovered Zeldin.

He became a perfect tool for them. At first they just used him as a toy that they could mock and tease, without getting any objection from the boy.

He, in turn, seemed to love the attention he was getting from this gang of older guys.

Later, he was honored by some of the same kids and given the task of delivering things for them. He would be given a package and an address. He ran to and fro, so that the guys would know he was working hard for them.

There another older kid would take the package and give him an envelope to bring back to his real friends. He had no idea as to the contents of the package or the envelope.

He generally did two or three trips each day and was rewarded with a few dollars for each trip. It was, undoubtedly, the most money he ever earned.

For at least years, I did not see nor hear of my Uncle Zeldin. Then he showed up at one of our family get-togethers.

Sophie's husband told me that he had just been released from Sing Sing Prison.

"They could have thrown him away for a much longer time, but the Judge, who was Jewish, had rachmunis for this simpleton and gave him a light sentence"

Two years later, I was told that Zeldin was dead. I didn't know how he died and just couldn't believe the rumors that he had committed suicide.

That night Momma and Poppa cried for Zeldin, a brother no one hardly knew.

Chapter Sixty-Four

The entire world knew that sooner or later the U.S. of A. would be totally involved in World War II. Everybody knew it would be a disaster, yet we did so with great gusto. The excuse was Japan but the reality of the situation was that we could not resist having Americans killed off in equal numbers as the remainder of the world.

I was only sixteen and, therefore, I could do nothing but both Buddy and Willie were soon drafted.

I assure you that Buddy was the quietest and most humble human being in all of that great army. He was very proud, if frightened, about doing his share in this war.

Three months after his induction, Buddy was in the middle of heavy Basic Training when the army, at the height of its stupidity, essentially ruined his life.

The first problem he faced was, that in the eyes of his Master Sergeant, who openly vented his hatred for Jews, there was nothing that Buddy could do correctly.

"Hey Jew Boy, is there anything you can do without screwing it up?"

Buddy just accepted the worst of it and learned to quietly do everything the Sergeant said, while knowing he would probably get screamed at for not doing it perfectly.

One night he was called out by said Sergeant with an order to take a guard position a few hundred yards into the forest that adjoined their current camp site.

"When you reach a huge rock, and I mean huge, stop there and be alert for anything that could mean trouble. Stay there for about three hours and then return to camp. Any questions?"

What in the name of hell was that supposed to teach him? I assure you Buddy just muttered 'No Sir. I got it.'

And off he went.

First off he didn't have a watch and, therefore, he had zero sense of what time it was, nor what time he was supposed to return to camp. In addition, the thought of marking the path he took never dawned on him.

He did strike out in the direction indicated by his Sergeant, but his search for that particular rock did not come easily. He walked and walked until he stumbled across a boulder that was rather large if not huge. Buddy guessed that it might seem huge to the Sergeant, so he took his position there and waited for time to pass.

For the longest period, not a soul came by. There was no moon in the sky, and the stars seemed to be covered with a heavy blanket of clouds.

He tried his best to guestimate the time, but gave up on that as a losing task.

For a short spell he did fall asleep and was awakened by the screeching of what he thought was an owl. He felt the time to return must have passed, so he started off back to camp.

He did so, despite the fact that he was totally covered with blackness. There was not one bit of light to guide him. The darkness surrounding him at that moment had grown even blacker and brought back to him another night of blackness that had severally wounded him.

The event had occurred a few nights after his eighteenth birthday, when the same sort of blackness had enveloped him.

He was coming home from work and decided to take a short cut home from the train station. This led him through many streets he rarely took.

He saw a light in the distance, so decided to head in that direction. Less than one minute later, he found himself flying through the air and down a flight of concrete stairs with its cover gates wide open.

His face was a mass of cuts and huge bruises, with blood falling down his face and coursing onto his jacket.

Somehow, he managed to crawl up the steps and, ever so slowly, found a way home.

Though there was no similar accident this night, the same chill coursed through his body as it did the night of the first accident.

Every way he looked, all he saw was blackness. The moon was totally hidden in heavy clouds. Not a star blinked away. Massive thickly limbed trees was a covering that could not be penetrated.

Heading back to camp was further complicated by the fact that he didn't have the least idea of where his camp was.

He couldn't see anything further away than five feet but knew he had to give a stab at getting back to his campsite.

After what seemed like days to him, but was just hours, he finally spied a road that looked familiar. An exhausting spell along that road finally revealed an army campsite.

Yes, it took him to a campsite, but not where his group was bivouacked.

"Halt. Who goes there?"

The human voice was most gratifying for Buddy who shouted as loud as he could, "It's me, Private Sinvalorvitz."

He then explained his being lost and his great desire to get to the right camp.

"Hey man it's just down that road but probably a good day's march away. If you can wait a couple of hours, we can drive you there.

It was not until late morning that he finally returned to his camp.

The first words he heard as he approached the center of camp was a roar from the Sergeant he reported to.

"Well look at this. Where the hell have you been?

Couldn't our little pussycat find his way home or were you trying to go AWOL on us? Sure that was it. You found out that we are scheduled to leave for Italy, so you decided to take a walk on us. You are a piece of garbage, and I am going to see that you pay heavy for this stunt."

Buddy tried to explain that he didn't know about Italy and it was just that he just couldn't see where he was.

"It was so dark that I kept getting more and more confused. I couldn't see a thing in the darkness and I ended up in a campsite miles from here."

"You little shit, I don't know what you're trying to pull off, but nothing smells right when you are involved."

This led to his being sent to the M.P. bivouac who viewed Buddy with the same skepticism as the Sergeant did.

They cuffed him and sent him to the doctor's quarters. The doctor who examined him was a gynecology specialist. His report gave added credence to what the Sergeant thought.

He strongly advised that Buddy be sent to see a reliable vision expert.

"That guy can better prove if this turd is a lying bastard, as the Sergeant thinks, or if he really does have a vision problem. Personally, I agree with the Sergeant that he is a no good bum who should be shot."

Buddy's fortune changed when he ended up in Washington D.C., where the army had more extensive doctors available.

It was the fifth doctor examining him before a decision was rendered which restored Buddy's credibility.

"Young man, I do believe you probably have a rare eye disease. I am sure you know what you have and that you can see just fine most of the time. But you are going to lose that battle. You'll be blind before you are thirty-five.

He then turned to his assistant and told him to just ship Buddy off to some Army office where he might be able to handle the chores without trying to get out of this war effort.

His final words to Buddy were, "Now get the hell out of my office."

In a period well short of six weeks, the Army had taken a man who believed in himself. . .who loved everything about life and what he was doing to help win this war...and decimated him.

The Buddy we knew was lost forever in that mass of people whose stupidity was beyond belief.

Talk about a ridiculous assignment. They placed him in an accounting office where he, with his vision problems, had daily opportunities to screw up everything he touched. No one ever determined, or cared, how good or bad he handled the job.

Nonetheless, his reputation had preceded him, and he was branded as one who tried to skip the job of winning this war.

He was, to all extents, a dead man. He did not make one friend in the three years he spent in the army. Any confidence or daring was gone forever.

His pre-army life which had been filled with the love of the pursuit of women was gone. His great desire to learn, while exploring intellectual matters, became a memory. Every justification he had about the worth of his being was left at the wayside.

He still had a few civilian friends and was at ease with his family, but he never achieved anything that might bring worth to himself.

We all suffered that loss.

Chapter Sixty-Five

Velvel was first assigned to a unit that was training for penetration into the German woods. As he told me on his first leave before shipping out to Europe, he was anxious to get on with it.

Then the Army, in its infinite wisdom, found that this soldier was a superb athlete. Soon thereafter, he was shipped out to Paris, France, where he was deployed to a group of basketball players who were assigned to entertain the real troops.

By the by, he was not home for the birth of his first child who was born three weeks after her father landed in France.

His being shipped to Paris would lead to a whole new chapter for the White family of New York City and the Pascal's of Paris.

Unbeknownst to any of us, our mother had given Velvel some names and an address that might lead to finding her long lost mother and her two brothers. She had harbored those addresses for many, many years.

As soon as he had a free day off, he wandered throughout every Jewish section of Paris. Being the best of our Yiddish speakers, he managed to go from one lead to another, but it was not until his third day searching did he discover a lead to the residence of a Jewish family named Pascal.

The letter we received detailed all he had found, yet did not present even a hint of joy in it.

It told us that we had a Grandmother and the wives of two uncles who lived in Paris in one tiny apartment with three little boys and two little girls.

Velvel's letter went on to tell of how old and, yet still courageous, Grandma Sarah had been in the telling of the tragedies they had endured. She also asked for nothing in return from Velvel.

She could not explain why she had allowed the two families to fall apart. Sarah's only rationale for the breakoff was simply the energy needed to survive the rigors of a growing family facing life in Paris.

Hitler had mounted a successful campaign into France and German soldiers and their French counterparts were jauntily using Paris as their little playground.

Somehow our Pascals had avoided the terror of the Nazis. Life went on, by hiding away from the new conquerors of their city.

But one night, our uncles had felt they could secure some milk for the family. Most of their shopping was done quietly and swiftly and when it was pitch dark.

Our newly found Grandmother told of pleading with her two sons that their children could easily survive the night without the seemingly mandatory cup of milk, but both of her sons replied that daytime was more dangerous than nighttime and they had already made the arrangements to get the milk.

Accordingly, the brothers left the safety of their home and ventured out for the milk.

They were never heard from again.

Momma broke down in tears at hearing that. She cried out that, no, it wasn't Sarah fault, it was Yettie's demand that her family quickly adjust to New York.

Probably, both mothers were equally to blame for not being more aggressive in maintaining some sort of relationship with each other.

Sarah told Willie that she was almost thankful when Grandfather Duvid Pascal died.

"Better that he quietly slipped away than keep suffering from disease after disease."

Momma told us much about this wonderfully handsome man who had an insatiable taste for life, only to have life turn its back on him.

In great detail she told us of the horrors he had sustained in Ellis Island.

The letter went on detailing that, in the past few years, death was expected by every Jew in Paris. To have the wives and children of her two sons survive was a miracle that left them the ability to go on with life.

Chapter Sixty-Six

Willie returned to the United States almost two years later. He was a changed man. He had a solidity about him that directed his every thought. It was far from easy for him to get the right job that could bring him some pleasure and allow him to support his wife and daughter as they deserved to be. Early in his return, we were having a festive dinner in celebration of his coming back to us.

Matty, with the devil's look upon her face, took up the subject of how welcoming the French women must have been to the marvelous U.S. soldiers who had restored their freedom.

Then she added a viscous sentence that was totally uncalled for.

"Tell me something, Willie, how did you get along with the French women?"

He was visibly furious, but in a gentle tone said that was a game that he had never entered.

"Oh come on. What about those two lonely widows you spent so much time with?"

To his credit he did not respond. Instead he gave a deep sigh and picked up his wife's and child's coats. He then nodded at Mom and me. Without a word, or a look at Matty, he took his family out of the apartment.

He never again said even one word to Matty.

I, on the other hand, immediately thought of Poppa and the word tolerance.

Outwardly, I couldn't have given a damn whether Willie had slept with every woman in Europe. I knew he adored his family. They were his life.

Inwardly, I knew no such event had occurred even once.

Chapter Sixty-Seven

I was fast asleep one Sunday morning when Momma tore into my bedroom. She had a very noisy battle with opening the lone window there.

Then she loudly proclaimed, 'Vay is mir is zer colt aher.'

My foggy head voiced many objections but my brain recognized some storm about to erupt.

I slowly opened my eyes and ears -- this little woman I called Momma voicing something akin to, 'end get up right now.'

The night before I had not been with my first true love. Instead I caroused with several of my buddies who were far better drinkers than I was.

'Nu, you vant to sleep the gonza took? It's already almost nine azager and you are slufing azoy a toitena.'

A yawn or two was all I could muster up as I desperately tried to find brain cells that were willing to function.

'Boichick, I got sumting I vant to freig dir.'

I weakly raised my head and nodded. I instantly knew it wasn't my sleeping that was bothering her but her wanting to know something and know it right away.

As I looked up at her she asked, 'Tell me somtik, vat's goink to be mit you and dat goil?'

No way of sleeping through such a question. I was suddenly wide awake. The question my mother posed could have awakened me from my deathbed. So my answer was quick and brief.

"Momma, I love her."

Her reply was epochal. With a big smile on her face she blurted out, *"You love her. So dats it and dats all."*

I leapt out of bed and gave Momma the biggest hug I could and more kisses than she had ever had.

I was right. She had determined that what she wanted to know was far more important than how much sleep I got that morning.

What a woman. She and my soon-to-be bride became the closest of friends and remained so to the very last day of my mother's life.

'Dat goil', Marnie, to all the remainder of the world, was the most perfect woman I had ever met. I knew almost from the first moment I saw her that she was the woman I wanted to share my life with. I must add that she was definitively not of the Jewish faith.

The good thing I had going for me was that Mom knew 'Dat Goil' had to be completely in love with me, since, in her eyes, everyone in the world was in love with me.

She heard my words 'I love her' and, with a big smile, said, "You love her. So dat's it and dat's all." I think that if 'dat goil' had been from Libia and only spoke in the Libian tongue, since I loved her, my Mom knew all would be fine for me.

It mattered not what others might say. Mom didn't give a hoot what anyone else thought. Whatever made me happy was just fine with her.

Being the typical male, I was always watching how my Mom and my bride-to-be got along. I knew all was well with the two of them when one day, while Mom was teaching her to make Salada de Venita, Marnie dared to query Mom with "Mom, don't you put radishes in salad?"

To which Mom responded. "If you got it, put it in."

Marnie continued this dangerous trespassing by saying, "What about cucumbers?"

"Didn't I tell you already? If you got it, put it in.'

Both Mom and Marnie had quickly formed an easy friendship. Mom made fun of Marnie's ever being able to cook a good Jewish meal and Marnie answered back by challenging Mom to try and make a dish called Rack of Pork with prunes.

Momma refused to be topped and sourly said, "Dat sounds like sometime I vud make fur an enemy.'

Their interchange was all the proof I needed that my mother and my wife-to-be would became the best of friends.

Other than Matty and her sour attitude, the rest of the family quickly fell in love with my lady.

Chapter Sixty-Eight

Unfortunately, a hitch did arise that made Mom capable of committing homicide.

Mom and the neighborhood women would, just about every summer evening, bring chairs out and then spread them across the sidewalk. Whether there were only two yentas seated there or fifteen a grand evening of 'yentering' would prevail.

Momma constantly regaled us with her stories of how she handled this very tough group of ladies who met every night in the middle of Brighton Beach Avenue.

Just sitting quietly was not in favor with this group. Arguing about everything was much more fun. Rarely did any of their talks end in any form of agreement.

One memorable evening their first argument was about who was a 'vois bastid, Hitler or Stalin.' It ended in a split decision.

A brief pause of about a few seconds quickly went by silently when Mrs. Finkelstein, a short and rather obese woman, uttered several loud 'oy vays.'

Without a doubt, Mrs. Finkelstein had for years been the self-appointed leader of what would be discussed each night. When she was gone from the group she was always referred to as the 'Fat Dictator.'

I had gotten home rather late and I was more than a little surprised to see Buddy, Momma and Poppa still sitting together at the kitchen table.

"Hey…Hello…I'm home. What's with you?"

"Dis man is always so nice, I get tired to talk on him".

"Vait. vait von minute. Your Mama tells me she is going to kill that Yenta, Mrs. Finkelstein. I say that woman deserves only von thing. Just don't listen to her. To her that is worse den dyink."

I tried to calm them down by asking to hear the entire story.

Momma and Poppa ignored me, but Buddy opened up the subject of what had transpired that evening by asking if those ladies were giving Mom a hard time about me and the new Tootsie I was parading around.

'Vat? You tink doz farstinkener Yentas could gif me trouble? Only Mrs. Finkelstein. Everyting was goink fine until dat rifka, Finkelstein, told me that she taut it was zer funny that mine boy's new goil friend looked like a shiksa. So I said, "Isn't dat funny. Den I asked her if she taut her fat son voud ever have a goil friend."

Momma did not add anything else, so I presumed the battle of the two tough Jewish women seemingly ended there.

At that point, Poppa cut off Momma and ordered me to sit down.

"Vot Momma left out was that she appened to have met George as she vas vorking home and she told him from what else vas said. And dat vas not da hole story. Nu, Molly, tell da boy what dat fastinkena momza really said."

(You might be wondering who the devil George is. Well, just hold your horses and you'll soon find out who George is and how he constantly saved our lives.)

"Vell, I was expecting her to shut up that fat mouth but no, she keeps going with 'Listen, Molly, I vouldn't care even if she vos a shevartza, but how come your delicious son goes mit a schiksa."

Poppa jumped in with, "Again mit only a half of the story?"

"All right. So I gave that courva a very dirty look picked up mine chair and walked away from those crazy Yentas."

"And you don't van to tell da boy dat also you tol George to geharget dat stupid woman. I told her dats silly. Just never talk to dat rifka again and she will suffer more from dat den from dyink."

The next night the chairs and stools were as usual drawn out one by one by the ladies.

Mrs. Finkelstein, as was her wont, arrived last and pulled out her stool. She opened it up and sat down and the chair instantly collapsed. She ended up flat on her back.

That event provoked a period of riotous laughter that seemed as if it would never stop. I mean can you picture that fat little lady flat on her back with her skirt high over her waist and therefore revealing her delightfully sparkled under pants.

Everyone wondered who had sliced each of the legs so that no one could sit on that chair.

Do you think it could possibly have been the work of George?

Chapter Sixty-Nine

If you were to tell Momma she was a woman of infinite compassion, and then explain what the word meant, she would laugh at you.

In reality, she was a loving, caring woman who knew what the world needed and tried to hand out healing powers to those who were in need of same.

Yes, very little wit or charm flowed forth from her, but deep down she was a wise woman who cared deeply for the welfare of everyone in the world, unless those people tried to bother anyone in her family.

I think she was most aware of what her daughter, Matty, kept hidden from us. Unfortunately, we all knew our sister had problems that constantly tore at her.

Be it late at night, or early morning, Matty was either on the phone or meeting with Mom, and Mom was always there for her tuchter who constantly was in need of help.

Momma was slowly aging when she phoned me early one Sunday morning, a very rare thing for her to do, and told me she had something important to ask of me.

That very night I took an early break from my home and went to have dinner at Mom's apartment.

Of course, Mom had whipped up some Potla Jela, as well as an additional bowlful for me to take home with me.

Momma's dictum was always first you eat and then you talk. That night the meal consisted of all the favorite food she knew I couldn't eat enough of.

I told her I loved every bite as I ate away, all the while knowing I was going to have to accept whatever she was about to ask of me.

A last wipe of the delicious rye bread into the olive oil soaked salad bowl and it was time to get to what she wanted to tell me.

'Listen mien sieser kint. You know dat I know dat you have the groisest hartz in da whole family. So I have to have you swear to do someting for me.'

I told her to ask away and it would be done.

She smiled at me and said it was easy for me to agree with her but it wouldn't be as easy to actually do what she asked.

"I vant your void that you vil loin from me how I take care auf Matty and ven I am gone… No, I vant you to start mit me right away."

The look on my face quickly revealed my distaste for what she had asked. I just kept looking at her but could not utter a word.

'You are now tinking dat I have said a dirty word. Vel you are wrong. Please do me one last favor and promise me dat you vil stay close to her. I know dat in your mind Matty means tsouris. You are right. But you are de only poison who can help her.'

"Mom, there is no way I can do that. Matilda listens to nothing but her tears. So why should she listen to me?"

"She vil listen to you because I vil tell her to do so and because she loves you very much"

Mom of course prevailed and I would soon be at Matty's beck and call.

I promised Mom I would do the best I could, all the while wondering why I had become 'Lucky Pierre.'

In the supposed plan, Momma would continue getting the serious problems, while I would handle all the silly ones.

Gradually the balance seemed to shift as more and more, I began to be the recipient of the tougher ones, as Momma was coasting by on the silly questions.

I went to Poppa and told him how I hated having those meetings with Matty.

When I said that I hated wasting my time being involved with all those stupid questions I was getting, he countered.

'Mine siesa kint di bist a stoma. Alla tug du entfer's einer fragas deiner Momma vaksen yinga'.'

Thus he blew me and my every stouris, by telling me that I was a dummy not to know that every question I responded to let Momma grow younger and younger.

The toughest problems I ever had to face were those that had no meaning to me.

She would tell me of a matter like this girl in her office who was a floozy and the men were going along with her scandalous behavior.

I didn't have the faintest clue as to how Matty or anyone else could counter that behavior, nor any of a dozen other similar behavior problems.

Mostly I would sit and listen to her as she took off on something that meant nothing to me. To be totally forthright most of my answers were inane.

The questions, or should we call them problems, were, in my mind, absolutely stupid.

I never understood how she was a part of our family. My father, my mother, my two brothers, and me, the little pisher, as they always called me, were formidable laughers, whereas she was always a carrier of the woeful parts of life.

Yes, Momma could come up with an answer like *'Zolst nisht geharget veren.'* Which translated into 'For such a sin nobody would kill you.'

An easy answer to any question that I sure as hell would have liked to have been able to use as one of my standard answers, but that just didn't ring true coming from my mouth.

Often Mom would walk away from one of the 'Matilda Talks' quite spent. Pop witnessed the end of one such session and immediately took me into the bathroom for a private talk.

I wondered if he was again going to teach me the best way to urinate. It was quite amusing with him seated on the closed toilet seat and me on the edge of the tub.

He surprised me when he started with the fact that Matty was causing a problem, and he felt I could help out in resolving her needs. He also intimated that Momma was handling the problems all by herself.

"Momma never lets on that this is tse fiel for her now."

I was tempted to tell him that he was a little bit late and that I had assumed that Momma had talked it all out with him prior to putting me to the fire.

Instead, I went along with his feelings about Momma. Never lying to Poppa, I had to tell him that I hated even the thought of trying to help Matty.

He broke out into one of his crazed laughs when he said, '*Who told you anyting from Mahtilda? I'm asking for your Momma. She is taka the von who needs help. Get her away from her tochta end I vill have my young froi back again.*'

Chapter Seventy

One afternoon Matty called and told me I had to meet with her and her famed psychiatrist the very next day.

I screamed NO for at least a half hour, but at ten forty-five the next day, purposely fifteen minutes late, I arrived at the shrink's office.

All was as pleasant as can be as she greeted me with a big hug and kiss, while the shrink thanked me for coming and advised me that my visit would help my sister immeasurably.

He droned on with much verbiage about how good a person Matty was but that she really needed my help to fend off the troubling days.

He continued on with her always having loved me and how important her family was to her.

"But you are the strength in your group. Matty has told me of how often you help your brothers, Buddy and Willy, but that you are quite cold to her. I hope you realize how much she needs you."

Now that was a blatant lie, for I spent at least an hour a day responding to her ever complicated needs or answering her query as to why my wife was never nice to her.

Of course, knowing how cruel Matty could be, and how my wife was at a loss on how to get closer to my sister, I merely nodded without any response. I let those comments slide by.

Instead, I brought in Momma's request that I be a companion for Matty and for me to have an open ear for all her needs.

"I've really tried, but I don't have the time nor the patience that Mom was born with. She is a perfect person, and I am not."

And here is where Matty lost it.

"Oh yes. Momma was perfect but the one time I brought a married man as my escort to one of your parties, you threw me out of your house. But that Momma could have a life-long lover never seemed to bother you. You know that she and Mendel, the boarder, went at it all the time."

I could not believe the words I had just heard. I do believe if I had a gun with me, I would have killed my sister and probably the shrink as well.

I felt like I had been hit with a sledge hammer. I leapt out of my chair screaming vile epithets at them.

I wanted to smash her face right then and there, as I kept remembering how wilted Mom was after each 'Matty' session.

I lost my cool and offered something like, 'You may think so, but to me that is a load of shit that you created to justify your nuttiness.'

I rose and took a very deep breath. It took me a good deal of time to stop glaring at the two of them. I was hurting so badly I couldn't talk. Finally, the following words came.

"Everybody in this room knows you made that up to justify your insanity. But, just for kicks, let's just say what you say is true. Whatever Mom did was Mom's concern and not for you or me to dirty that wonderful woman with. It was her life. She made my life and Pop's and Buddy's and Willie's life a total joy. And if I ever hear you say those words again, I will beat you silly."

I then pulled out a hundred dollar bill and threw it at the shrink. I nearly tore the door open as I sped off. I do not know what I said other than I became as terrible as they were. I do confess to being as foul-voiced as possible. And the words I included were some of the worst in my vocabulary.

As I opened the door I spun back to Matty and spit out to her, 'Momma died every day worrying about you and she passed that burden on to me. You should be ashamed at what you just said, but, then again, it is typical of the way you operate.'

I cannot remember much of what else came forth but I recall shouting out as loud as I could, "She was an angel, and you are a slut."

I can't recall anything else happening that day. I just wandered from one street to another avenue. I didn't have a clue as to whether I slept at home or not. I know I did not eat nor drink until the following day.

Chapter Seventy-One

It took a full year before I even thought of how Poppa would have handled the situation.

I knew that I must establish some kind of relationship with Matty. Without a doubt, she needed my wife and my kids. I rationalized that she at least deserved that joy as she had no one else. The kids brought happiness to her, and she lavished love all over them at every opportunity she got.

In typical Matty manner, it was overly effusive and upon her leaving our house the kids would be all over me, demanding that I get her to lay off on the hugs and the kisses.

I could have lifted him in joy when my six year old son said Aunt Matty was very hard to be with and my four year daughter agreed, parroting that she didn't like Aunt Matty.

Instead, I played the good parent saying she has had a tough life so we have to help her.

I did not respond to the mutually spoken, 'Why?'

The toughest problems I ever had to face were brought to me by my sister. She was married and divorced twice, there was nothing positive in her life, other than never ending despair.

Our mother was my sister's constant advisor and defender, but that wise woman knew her limitations. Whenever I saw Mom and my sister head to head, I knew my sister was looking for easement from some imagined sin she committed or was about to be committed on her.

It was without doubt but that Mom would end the debate with some great Yiddish expression that my father thought was apropos for the situation.

"I don't know how long anyvone can keep up with dat tsores. Even Moses could not have come up mit answers for Matilda."

The truth of the matter as to why I so detested Matty goes back to one day when I was a young kid.

I was in third or fourth grade when I walked in to the living room where Matty and two of her friends were having a grand old time. She and the girls she was with had been screaming and laughing for some time. You should know that it was called the living room only during the day while at night it was Matty's bedroom.

As I neared them my sister grabbed me and put me on her lap and then rubbed me up and down her lap while she and the other girls giggled away. I didn't know what was going on but I knew I was not pleased to be treated in this manner. It took me many years before I could realize that I had been their little sex toy.

To this day, I recall how angry I was with all three girls. I could hardly wait for the next day which was Poppa's Sunday off.

As soon as I got up I raced to the kitchen, where Poppa was immersed in the Sunday Mirror.

In essence, I pulled the paper out of his hands as I shouted, 'Poppa, why does Matty make me hate her so much?'

He looked at me, neatly folded the paper he was reading, and with a puzzled look on his face, asked how I could hate her when she was always telling him how much she loved me?

"Since I really like the word love and don't like the word hate maybe you should decide who is right or wrong in how you feel about your svesta."

I was thoroughly confused. My mouth was agape, as Poppa's words started to sink into my brain.

How was I supposed to like this person whose every action struck me as being dreadful? I never really liked Matty, but my father, whose every word I adored, kept telling me that my hatred for her must disappear and be replaced by something called love.

Well Poppa's words were on a par with a message from God, so for the rest of my life I tried to follow his advice. My trying to be a friend to this terribly confused woman called my sister never did come about. For me, it was impossible to do.

Chapter Seventy-Two

By now you are probably aware that I used my father, my Poppa, as my personal encyclopedia. No, I didn't ask him how to spell words, as he didn't have a clue about spelling and couldn't care less about it.

I constantly was prodding him for answers on how a young man should live his life.

The questions were ever forthcoming. Answers were rarely offered.

Truth be told, not once did he really answer any question. But he would lead me to discover the answer myself.

Sometimes he would answer with a long story about Iasi. Let me give you an example.

"Pop, I've got a problem."

"You've got a problem...you little pisha, you don't know from vat dat void means. Mine mother, ven I was ten years old and still living in Iasi found out that Dieter, who you were named after, was not Jewish."

His head began to shake back and forth then up and down. *"Now dat voz a problem. I took care of it mineself. Start thinking and you vil come up with yur own answer."*

When he added, 'De Ha'kn mir a chinik', I knew he didn't have a clue on how to answer me and, more importantly, I should figure it out myself.

Whenever he was slightly uncertain on how to answer me, he took me deep into Yiddish with expressions like that which literally said, 'stop banging on the tea kettle, you are giving me a headache.'

Very rarely would he give me a real answer, but he would often pick up a good word or sentence I would proffer, twist the words around a bit and, voila, offer up what sounded like a good solution.

When he was totally unaware of what I was talking about, he had another standard reply which was also answered in Yiddidish, 'Gay frage der poleashe mensch frim de gas.'

Which I knew that was his way of telling me to get lost. What else could 'Go ask that question from the police man on the corner' mean?

The fact that I never got any direct help from him did not in any way dissuade me from coming right back for more of his answers to my often bewildering queries.

Of course, he did offer up clues as what path to take in solving the problem, but it was invariably offered up as a Jewish Joke. When he finally had me laughing hysterically, I knew I was close to having my 'umglik' misfortune being solved.

His oft-repeated favorite was a conversation between two very wise Rabbis. They were discussing the forthcoming marriage between Arthur Miller and Marilyn Monroe. One Rabbi offers up a sarcastic remark "Ah, I don't give it a year." The other Rabbi replies: "Aza yohr oif mir."

Translation: '*I should have such a year.*'

And, what he really was saying was, look for the good in the problem and you will find the correct answer.

Early on, I realized that he was teaching me how to think. I guess I was learning something far more valuable than how to get an answer to some inane question. Of course, of even greater worth, was that there were always two or three great laughs that I took away from each of those sessions.

My Mom didn't have the slyness of my father and not a hint of his wit, but she, too, worked hard at teaching me how to think. Her answers were always direct and to the point but without even a hint of humor. She had the answer to any question I might pose. She was the most direct person I ever met.

I was about ten when I first met George. Yes, that George.

A mighty storm had charged right out of the Atlantic Ocean and smashed through the four windows that faced out from my parents' bedroom. The entire room was a disaster area.

The following day was quite nice which allowed Mom to clean up a bit of the mess. She knew better than to ask for any help from my father. That was not in his repertoire, so Mom had to seek help from others.

She decided that we needed someone who could really handle all the damage that almost had destroyed our apartment.

Per usual, when my mother set out to do something, one should consider it done. Within two blocks from our building, she ran into Flossie, the young black woman who on occasion cleaned our house.

Mom advised Flossie of her desperate need to get someone to clean up the mess in our house. Five minutes later, Flossie rushed up the stairs dragging along her latest boyfriend, George.

By the time I got home for lunch most of the cleaning was nearly done.

Mom insisted that all work stop and she prepared lunch for the four of us. It was a gala affair. More importantly, when I came home from school at three-thirty, Flossie and George were gone and the house looked just as it did before the storm hit.

"Wow, I proclaimed, I bet it cost a ton to get this done so fast."

"Not so much. But I made a deal mit George dat he liked. From Flossie I do not know. They vil come vonce a week and fix what has to be fixed, and I vil make a lunch like they never had before."

George was as funny and as nice as can be, but, as Mom pointed out to me, Flossie soon got a better job, and George brought over a new girl to replace her.

For the next ten years we always had a girl that George got for us and at a price that Mom could afford.

Whenever George came to our house to fix something, he would see me and immediately ask me a question like 'What's cookin chickin?'

George's expertise was in two areas, both of which I was a total failure at. The first was fixing broken things. I still cannot even drive a nail straight into a wall.

The second area led to even greater failures. He was a magician in the handling of women, while I was a complete buffoon at that game.

He quickly became my fourth tutor behind Pop, Mom and Buddy.

Chapter Seventy-Three

Jim Valvano, the famed and brilliant college basketball coach at North Carolina State also challenged the world with wonderful words.

He was invited to deliver the keynote address at the 1993 Espy Awards Dinner Earlier that year he had been informed that he had contracted mastic cancer and he would not have much time before he would succumb to that deadly disease. He insisted upon giving the speech.

His major quote that night is still used as an inspirational tool.

That now famed quote stated the credo my father, Buddy and Willie, patterned their lives after.

"There are three things you must do every day. The first of those is to laugh; the second is to think, and the third is to cry."

Two months after speaking those monumental words, Jim Valvano died.

I never could figure out how he, my father and my brothers could formulate the same life pattern.

Bless you, Coach Valvano.

Chapter Seventy-Four

Buddy and Velvel deserve further words for the way they lived their lives.

I heartily suggest you join me in getting out your handkerchiefs because whenever I bring those vunderkints up, I usually break out with tears flowing down my cheeks. But here goes.

Buddy, was the sweetest, kindest man ever to inhabit this earth. Yes, he was the winner of the contest for the healthiest baby in the lower east side. I think he won that award because he probably smiled his way through all the testing. He kept smiling for the whole of his life.

My first memories of Buddy were about my wanting to be near him because he always made me feel so good. Not once, in all our years together, did he do anything but praise me and boost my ego.

He backed me no matter what I tried. There wasn't an event in my life where he wasn't up front, praising me to the skies.

Be it my bar mitzvah boocha days, when he told me that no one had ever given such a speech as well as I did, which was one of the few lies he ever told, to my going to college, to my marrying Marnie, to my opening my own business, yes to everything I touched, he was there with limitless encouragement.

It wasn't until my really maturing that I realized that he desperately wanted me to be successful, because his life was filled with failure.

Of course, the Army doctor's prediction about his losing his sight did come true.

With it came his being fired from Cagans, one of the toniest men's clothing stores in town. He had worked there since before joining the army and then again upon being discharged. He had been one of the most successful salesmen on the floor.

The owners of the store adored Buddy but, bit by bit, came to realize that Buddy's mistakes were more serious than just little errors.

Coincidentally, Marnie and I were leaving our first apartment. It was inexpensive which allowed Buddy, for the first time in his life, to leave the family dwelling. He took over our old apartment and enjoyed this new found freedom.

Things had gone well for me, and it was not a burden for us to see that all his expenses were covered.

Having his own place was a major boost to his self-esteem. So much so, that he got a job doing the books for a small hardware store which was close to the apartment. Oddly enough he seemed capable of handling the eye problem of deciphering figures.

Six months later those nice people had to send Buddy on his way.

He was now legally blind, and any ego-restoring job was out of the picture.

Despite the agonies that came hand in hand with his being blind, there also reigned an attitude that was nothing short of remarkable. He never stopped believing in himself.

He and I might be strolling down Fifth Avenue and, as usual, he would lead the way, with his cane swinging wildly from right to left.

I begged him to contain the cane, as he was coming very close to hitting those walking by us, and he laughingly told me that he was helping the other walkers to be more alert on this crowded street.

It was said with a hearty laugh.

Years passed and Marnie and I had decided to move from the city to Aspen, Colorado. That plan was heartily endorsed by Buddy.

We told Buddy that we were going to build a four-bedroom home. The bedrooms would go to each of our two children, ourselves and Buddy.

He was more than delighted by the thought of joining us away from the turmoil of New York.

Three weeks before he was to move to Aspen, he suffered a heart attack. The doctors forbade his moving there because of its altitude.

I am uncertain as to whether they were right or wrong, but for the next ten years he visited us in Aspen many times. He then moved to Santa Monica, and shortly thereafter we joined him there.

The first Sunday after we arrived he walked the seven blocks from his house to our house. That Wednesday he had another heart attack. I reached the hospital minutes before he died.

Chapter Seventy-Five

Willie's life was far less dramatic than that of Buddy. He was eleven years younger than Buddy but full of spirit to conquer the world. He had a good wife, a beautiful baby and the energy to really go for it in this trying world of ours.

Upon returning from the Army, he decided to open a low cost bakery in a slum area. He felt that such a store would be a big hit that he could eventfully open throughout the city.

Unfortunately, he soon found that his customers did more stealing of his goods than purchasing them.

His next venture led him to a sales job with the Sunshine Biscuit Company. It was a good pairing for both him and the company. For most of the years with the company he was their 'numero uno' in sales.

To his after-the-fact regret, he started an effort to unionize the company. This failed effort only led to his being fired.

Hardly daunted, he soon was hired by The Associated Press selling the unusual photos they had available.

He was a monstrous success at that job. Things could not have been better. Once again, he was the top salesman in the company

Poppa used to say, "Dat mensch dat people call GOD made up doz bubamonsas that the hole voild loves and I say is for stoomies."

That same 'holy' person decided to spill feces over Velvel and his family.

Wasn't Buddy going blind enough for one family? Obviously not. Willie's eye power began to disappear rapidly. He had not told a soul about his eyes going bad on him.

Within four years, he was as blind as Buddy. How or why they contracted Retinitis Pigmentosa is still a mystery.

His career with Associated Press was ended. However, they were more than gracious with Willie when they terminated his career. He was given a handsome retirement benefit which kept his life as financially secure as feasible.

No, not a rich man but, yes, a man who never had to worry about the little money he needed for the remainder of his life.

He thought of a million different things he could do to earn a living but no one would hire him.

His troubled life was further complicated as an odd thing was taking over his life. He had a loving wife who in essence became his eyes. She took over parts of his life that were better left to him alone.

As a consequence of the help she provided, he became less independent than Buddy. Yes, he could still get up on a stage and harangue a huge group of people into donating funds for the Fight Blindness Campaign, but he couldn't walk downstairs to buy the local paper.

They moved to the warmth of Florida and were having a fun time there. If you were to ask him what kept him so busy his standard reply was always the same.

"I have to go to the Supermarket and watch the trucks unload. They couldn't do it without me being there."

This great athlete, this man who loved laughing at the world, this grand raconteur, this dancer extraordinaire was parlaying all of this into a world of joy.

He probably had the greatest reward possible by the success of a charity he helped found. Of course all the Funds raised went into research for the blind.

He had always been a fine dancer, so one day he decided to open a folk dance class for his neighbors. I recall sitting in on one of those lessons and having to stuff a handkerchief in my mouth so that I wouldn't burst out in screaming laughter.

Willie would be in front of a dozen old and fat women, as he shouted out the moves to be made. Now you know he was blind and all the women were in back of him.

Despite all, he would shout out things like, 'SADIE IT'S YOUR RIGHT FOOT FIRST. YOUR RIGHT FOOT.'

Sometimes he would curse them in Yiddish and their response would be hearty laughter.

And how was he repaid for all the good work he did?

He took sick one day. He was only sixty-one so we weren't worried about him. Three days later he was taken to a hospital.

The following day I received an urgent call from his daughter saying that he had taken a turn for the worse so, of course, I immediately flew to visit with him.

Nobody would tell me exactly what disease he was suffering from. His doctor, in the few seconds I met with him, merely said he wouldn't last long.

As we left his room after a full afternoon of his doing nothing but lie there with his eyes closed, we all started to leave. I was the last one to go.

I took about fifteen steps before turning back and reentered the room. I bent over him and put my lips right on his left ear.

I very softly whispered, "Willie, I love you."

I swear to the heavens above I heard him say, "I love you too."

Willie died that night shortly before midnight.

Chapter Seventy-Six

I took the attitude that one day I too would lose my sight. But to this day my eyes have retained their strength.

Each of them were as hard working as I. They were far brighter. And, oh how they could laugh. The reality of it all was that I couldn't top them at anything. Yet I became the successful one.

I never understood the why of what happened to them had ignored me. I often wondered whether my brothers hated me for my good fortune. I never heard one thing that would justify that concern.

I was always proud of Buddy and Willie. They never stopped being the best friends and supporters I ever had.

I went through early childhood, then the crazy teens, into college and then adulthood. But, for Matty, and even there I knew she loved me, I never received anything but plaudits from my entire family.

That resulted in a man that totally believed in himself. Oh sure, I failed at many things and had doubts of my having taken a correct path here and there, but I believed I was a good guy.

The best thing I had going for me was the wonderful examples I had to base on what kind of a man I would be.

Poppa laughed at life. This despite having to face the bullets of having no money being fought every day. Even more of a continuing battle was the need to keep a brave face in front of his family at all times.

I do believe Momma set an even better example for me. She was the ruler of the family and her daily handling of eternal worries was a wonder to see. A problem arose, and she would face up to it, and in some form or other defeat the problem.

Willie and Buddy sure had every reason to complain about what they faced. But I never heard one of them utter a single complaint about being blind. Instead they used every tool at their command to cope with what they had and never needlessly burdened anyone with his need for self-pity.

But I probably learned the most from Matty. She was stricken from birth with the ever begging want to have someone take care of her.

She was fearful of everything and had little to no self-regard. Consequently, the world responded with having her face agony after agony.

Actually Momma's forcing me to care for Matty was yet another brilliant move on Momma's part. It, in the long run, taught me to appreciate how well off I was.

Just starting to listen to Matty changed my entire perspective of her. She was more to be pitied than scorned.

Yes there were days when I wanted to give her a good boot in the ass, but more and more I tried to appreciate that to her life had been one disaster followed by another.

Chapter Seventy-Seven

And Poppa took the spotlight again.

I was living in Phoenix, Arizona while working for Paramount Pictures and as lonely as any man has ever been. Poppa saved me by his weekly missives to me.

Would that I could present them all to you but time has weathered them and they are barely decipherable.

I have selected one that is somewhat readable. I hope you will see in these words the inherent humor and wisdom that flowed from that man.

I had to translate much of his writing so don't despair as you will certainly have definitive troubles with much of his 'wordsmanship.'

I once asked him how long it took him to write me those letters and he told me that he only wrote on the Sundays he didn't go to work. Between his letter writing and his Daily Mirror he was fully occupied those days.

I swear to you that what follows is far from the most outlandish letters he wrote. Hopefully, you will enjoy the trips that Poppa took me on. I've enlarged the type face for that's the way he wrote. God forbid you couldn't see one of the words he had written to you.

Dear Bum.

Last night me and Momma and Abey vent to see Menasha Skulnick tanks to Abie's dollars. In plain English the play was fakakta drek.

Your Momma took along her new teet vich are getting to be the most expensive ting we have.

Ve come home almost at tvelve o'clock. I vuz zer tired and dona Momma was more crankavotta den usual. She took a sleeping pill and I took a hot bag to hold against my tuchas.

Momma is having lunch mit doz strange friends of her. I am sure she will shlep along the teet to show them how vel off ve are. Also she is afraid to leave the teet at home.

Momma looks good, I am still retired and still vaiting to get a break from Vall Street.

I hope you are showing everybody what a smart mench you are. Also, vat would be so bad if they brought you bek to New York so ve could see you?

If you like I can talk to Mr. Hyman and tell him dat his company needs a smart guy like you right here.

Ve are villing to give you a ittle more time with the goyim but ve are not spring tsikens and vould like to see you more den every other yuntif.

Momma kisses your picture. I miss telling you how the vorld shud be run.

She misses you more than you can believe and I keep vaiting for you to come to me and ask me a question that has no answer.

Abie is Abie. Velvel is Velvel. Mathilda is still a pain in the tuchas.

Mit much love we send our kisses.

Momma and Poppa

Chapter Seventy-Eight

I opened this book by saying hello.

I hope you have enjoyed learning about the family that I introduced you to half as much as I enjoyed writing it.

Since starting this book, I have known that I must reserve the following chapters as its finale.

I have been told that one tries never to end a book on a down note, and, God knows, two deaths are not exactly a stroll through the park.

But I view the following as a tribute to two of the finest people that ever trod the pathways of this world.

I was twenty eight when I lost my father. A doctor was called in to somewhat calm me down. I couldn't breathe...I couldn't talk...I couldn't stand.

The doctor, bless his soul, did nothing but chat with me for a solid hour, and I slowly recovered even though I cried non-stop for about ten hours.

I am certain that Poppa was worshipped by all of our family and tears do eventually dry up but, to this day, the mere thought of his name still opens a floodgate of tears that race down my cheeks.

Momma was the bravest of us all. No she didn't have much to say, and, yes, she shed a ton of tears.

She knew that Poppa's departure meant that she must be more of a leading mother than ever before. She was remarkable in fulfilling that position.

When he was sixty-four she had told Poppa that she needed him to spend more time with her and that it was now time to tell his bosses that he was thinking about retiring.

Within the next few months he met with his bosses and told them that he would like to retire when he turned sixty-five.

His bosses were in accord with that plan, but they did nothing about filling the creative void his departure would create.

At that same time, he had asked them if he could drop by once in a while to spend a little time with his good friends the two Italians he had hired and taught the art of tailoring. The bosses agreed to same.

He also asked if they got too busy and might need another tailor could they consider him for a day or two of work. They seemed to nod their heads to that as well.

For Poppa the months flew by and, true to his word, on his sixty-fifth birthday he did retire. He never let on to anybody, not even Molly, how trying it was to do so.

Not even on his very last day on the job did the bosses acknowledge that this man had spent most of his life working for their father and them. They did not even wish him well in his retirement.

His two fellow tailors, the once young Italians he had tutored in the art of tailoring, openly cried as he turned to them.

"I vant you two to know that even though you are not Jewish, I vil still miss you. And remember, better to have the cuffs too long than too short."

They both hugged and kissed Poppa. They couldn't say a word, for they were fighting to retain the tears that threatened to overwhelm them.

They cowered and offered not one word. On turning from Poppa, they kept their eyes glued to the floor.

Poppa quietly strolled through the store and out the front door.

Poppa jumped into retirement. His unique way of betting on the horses increased to almost a daily occupation.

I offered to give him real money to invest in his job, but he turned me down cold.

"Vat are you talking. If I put your money in my silliness and I lose, I am no longer having fun mit my craziness."

He loved to walk to the beach front and became a constant searcher for odd shells.

His most fun was from taking a mid-morning train ride to the shop he had worked in for over forty years.

Mostly, he would just talk to his old fellow tailors. Occasionally, he would see an old customer. That always turned into pleasant conversations.

Very rarely the bosses asked him to put in a half days work. That would be the highlight of his days.

After the first of those days, he told me, "And you know something, I vas as good as ever. I never lost a stitch."

This all fell apart when Poppa went to the shop on a Saturday which usually was the busiest day of the week.

When he entered the store there wasn't a single customer to be seen. He quietly stole to the back of the store where his old fellow workers sat.

As he entered that room he asked Angelo, "Nu vots mit Tony? Ver is dat bum?"

Angelo very sadly advised Poppa that things were so slow now that they only needed one tailor on Saturday, and they didn't open any longer on Sundays.

It was at this point that the older brother of the two who owned the shop stormed into the room.

He screamed at Poppa that he could no longer come to the shop. "This is a business not a gossip shop."

He went on in the vilest of words to berate my father as being a bad influence and disruptive. He then ordered Poppa out of the shop immediately.

I have not included any of the off-color words he shouted at my father.

Poppa quietly stole out of the store.

In later talks, he told me that he got to a little park down the street. He sat down on a close-at- hand bench and broke down. He had never been so hurt in all his life. He sat there for about an hour crying for every second of that hour.

Somehow he managed to get on the subway and got home.

When he reached our building, he sat down on the couch in the entranceway. He never rose from that couch but sat there crying for at least two hours before Momma, coming home from seeing an afternoon movie, entered the lobby and there was her love, her Schmuel, sitting on the couch crying.

The sight nearly killed my mother.

My father never returned to being the man he had always been.

Exactly six months later, as he neared sixty six, when, one very late night, Momma heard him walking from the bedroom. She asked if something was bothering him, and he told her he wasn't feeling well. She told him to take an Aspirin, smoke a cigarette, and go back to bed.

He did just that.

Early the next morning Momma got up and saw that Poppa was turned to the wall and very quiet. She tiptoed out of the bedroom and did not return to it until she realized it was ten o'clock, and she hadn't heard a word from Poppa.

Considering that his normal rising time was between five-thirty and six, she was frightened silly.

She called to him several times before she acknowledged what had happened.

Her Schmuel had died.

I am certain that I was the only one who knew that his being viciously thrown out of his working place in that dreadful manner was the cause of his death.

Do I believe that he was sentenced to death on that terrible day? Yes, with every bone in my body, I know that man could have shot him in the heart and not hurt my father more than his words did.

They first had killed the business that their father and my father had built and then killed the star of that business, my Poppa.

Chapter Seventy-Nine

Momma was beyond belief. Oh yes, she grieved, but, no, she didn't go crazy. She tended to her children knowing how badly we were hurting.

To her credit, Matty spent most of the time tending to Momma.

But my father's passing was so difficult for me to handle that I nearly lost the desire to continue with my life. I went through every laugh he had given me and every solemn idea he had bequeathed to me.

Momma changed all my thinking about living and dying as she told me how much Poppa loved life and the thought of death had never become a part of his vernacular.

It wasn't but three months after Poppa's death that I received a Saturday night call from Momma. She told me that she wanted to visit Poppa the very next day.

I must admit to being a bit thrown back by that request, but her every word was my command so Sunday morning at ten-thirty, I arrived at her front door.

I must confess that I felt this would be a one-shot trip. Instead, I came to enjoy Momma and me visiting Poppa's gravestone just about every two months or so.

As we slowly traveled out to the cemetery, Momma would mostly discuss how my family was doing and the good and bad of each of my children.

Our limited conversation always ended with Momma saying I was a lucky gonif to have such a fine wife and children who were absolutely perfect.

With that she would never say another word until I parked the car some fifty feet away from Poppa's gravesite.

This was a very popular Jewish cemetery, and Momma would spend much time looking at the hundreds of small stones that were gathered around Poppa's grave.

Then she would ever so slowly advance toward Poppa's grave. She would stop every few feet and pick up three little stones from the path we were on.

She would then kiss each of the stones as she separately placed each one on Poppa's gravestone. This was some ancient Jewish tradition which somehow sent greetings to the other world.

Momma would then seem to mumble something to my father. All would be quiet and then Momma would shout up the skies, "Vy did you leave me?…Vy did you leave me?…Vy did you leave me?...

Yes, she ended each of our visits to Poppa by crying out to who knows who, 'Vy did you leave me?'

She would then turn to me and say. "It's time to go home."

She never said another word until I opened the car door in front of where she lived. She would then gently kiss me and tell me to drive carefully on my way home.

Chapter Eighty

Let me next recount the most difficult night of my life.

I had gotten home rather late from a very busy and not very profitable work day.

Normally, I would phone Buddy and then check out Willie's number.

Matty was next and my final call always went to Mom, and it always was a pleasure.

How I loved that woman. She would tell me everything that had happened to her that day. It was usually a repeat of the conversation we had had the day before, and I loved every minute of her remarks.

These calls was set in concrete, and I never changed the order in which the calls were made. For whatever reason, that night I had actually started to make those calls, but I was dead tired and irritable about a tough work day, so I didn't dial any of them.

Pure self-indulgence of course.

It was less than an hour later that Willie, who lived half a block away from Momma, called me. He hit me right in the nose with the fact that Momma had had a heart attack and died.

His message came through faintly, but I could feel the tears covering the words. I told him I would get to Buddy and Matty and, hopefully, be at his house with them as quickly as I could.

But first I bent my head into my desk and wept and wept, and wept. My heart had just been broken. The woman I loved with all my soul had been taken away from me.

All too soon, at the age of seventy-two, my Momma, the love of my life, had left me to face this so trying world of ours.

Eventually, I called Buddy and passed the news on to him. He wasted no tears on his feelings but instead told me how we must handle Matty.

Talking with him was very difficult, for he had loved Mom far more than all the rest of us.

We agreed that I would first pick him up, and then we would get Matty and try to ease her into this awful news.

I somewhat pulled myself together and flew to Buddy's home. We did not talk of Mom's death but how to keep Matty from going crazy.

Essentially he told me that we've got to be cool about this so that we could somehow control the massive hysteria Matty would certainly go through.

He was more than right. It was almost midnight when I rang her front door bell.

A moment or two went by before Buddy shouted out it was us and would she please come to the door.

Her response came in a scream of the word 'Momma.' Even with the door closed, we were certain she knew why we were there.

Matty peered out, as the door slowly opened. She espied us and all her fears were transmitted without a word being spoken. She collapsed to the floor as she screamed out, 'Momma, Momma.'

We slowly gathered her up. I could not get a word out but Buddy became a healer and, ever so slowly, she settled down.

An hour later, we got to Momma's apartment. Her body had already been removed and further doings had been set between the funeral home and Willie. He had done a magnificent job.

Then he revealed what Momma's next door neighbor had told him about what had happened that night.

It seems Momma had gone to her neighbor for what he presumed was a bout of some pre-bed-time yentering.

She spent about twenty minutes there and then said she had to go back to her place because her son, Dietie, always called her every night about that time.

Momma walked the few feet to a couch in her foyer which had a phone at its side.

A few moments later her neighbor took some trash out to the garbage room. As she walked by Mom's apartment she noticed the front door was open so she peeked in.

Momma was sprawled out half way on the couch and half way on the floor. She was obviously dead.

The vision that spun before me was my wondrous mother racing to take my phone call. A call I had not made because I was such a lazy, self- indulgent bastard. Once again I could not stem the tears.

This miserable human being who was too tired to talk to his mother nearly collapsed in abject pain.

I have spent hundreds of moments reliving that night. I have always hated myself for the call I did not make.

I refused to let anyone even think of selling the couch she had died on. To this day, it is the most valuable piece of furniture in our home As I write these words, the wound in my heart reopens.

I reserve the right to cry for my wonderful Mom and the Bastard I was.

Chapter Eighty-One

Momma, Poppa, Buddy and Willie remain alive in my heart. I derive great pleasures being with them. Matty is alive and fighting a series of illnesses. I care for her with much pity. She never learned to enjoy life as all of us Sinvalorvitz's did.

I hope you appreciate the other members of your family as well as I do. Furthermore, I hope you write about your days with your family.

Writing about the people I loved, and the adventures they lived through, has given me hours and hours of pleasure.

It is time for me to say farewell. I leave you with two thoughts. First the words of Jim Valvano and then Poppa's way of saying Good Night.

"Every day you most do three things. The first thing is to laugh. The second thing is to think and the third thing is to let your emotions turn to tears."

"Ich lieb die azoy ful. Zai frailach und lach allar gonsa tug."

Or in his new tongue, I love you so much. Stay happy and laugh all day every day of your life.

Lexicon

Aller tuk	Every day
Ashkenazie	Jewish Sect
Bek	Back
Brillin	Eye Glasses
Brika	Bridge
Ba mir bist du Schein	By me you are pretty
Benken Dir	I beg you
Crankavota	A very cranky woman
Dona	Your
Familia	Family
Fakata drek	Feces
Foist	First
Gib a gries fin mir	Give her my best
Ginik	Enough
Gitten	Good
Goyim	Christians
Greiz	Mistake
Groiser	Big, Great
Hoich	Tall
Ich chub fargessen	I have forgottten
Ich zein alles	I see everything
Kenisht	Doesn't know or cannot
Kleine	Small
Poifec	Perfect
Redin	Speak
Richtik	Real
Roiter or Rota	Red
Schlep	Carry

Printed in the United States
By Bookmasters